The Dance of the Blue Crab

Marie Trotignon

iUniverse, Inc.
New York   Bloomington

The Dance of the Blue Crab

iUniverse books may be ordered through booksellers or by contacting:

iUniverse
1663 Liberty Drive
Bloomington, IN 47403
www.iuniverse.com
1-800-Authors (1-800-288-4677)

ISBN: 978-1-4401-9036-0 (pbk)
ISBN: 978-1-4401-9037-7 (cloth)
ISBN: 978-1-4401-9038-4 (ebk)

Printed in the United States of America

iUniverse rev. date: 11/13/2009

Dedication

✾

To my incomparable, steadfast travel companions and the unforgettable adventures we've shared.

Acknowledgements

❀

My very special thank you to Harry McIntyre, Robert Ross, Ethel Winter and Jo Olason, members of the Seahurst Writers whose support, encouragement and constructive critiquing helped bring this book together.

Prologue

❀

During courtship, in order to entice the female out of hiding, the boy crab performs a wild, provocative dance known as the "blue crab boogie."
New Scientist 7 April 2008

CHAPTER ONE

Well, it certainly wasn't a place she'd have chosen for a vacation. That is, if she'd been given a choice. Which, obviously, she hadn't. Marla glared disdainfully about the small, dimly lit room. Definitely not what she'd expected after hearing Naomi's gushing description of her brother's "adorable" cottage. Just one more faulty glitch, Marla decided, in what was proving to be a disastrous mistake rather than a vacation.

The entire plan had gotten off to a bad start. Naomi, Reba and Marla, a history of a close friendship behind them, usually tried to arrange their vacation time so they might travel together. They'd shared some great trips, some wonderful adventures. This year Marla proposed they visit Spain. She even took an evening class in conversational Spanish. Then, at the last minute Naomi dumped her surprise. Her brother, Ed, offered the use of his Cape Cod cottage, rent free, for two weeks. Marla was less than enthusiastic; she'd really been looking forward to visiting Spain. Congenial, easy going, Reba really didn't care, but Naomi, the more pragmatic of the three, was nearly beside herself with this unexpected windfall.

"It'll be such fun," she insisted. "Ed's place isn't far from a quaint little New England fishing village where we can poke around to our hearts' content. Just think, no hassles with unreliable trains, over-crowded planes and space available standbys. Just walking the beach every morning, watching the sunset every evening."

Naomi, Reba and Marla were all employed in some phase of the travel industry so the thought of no frustrating, time-wasting standbys held a definite appeal. But for Marla, the lure of prowling the beaches cinched it. Of course, based on their previous travel experiences, Naomi knew that.

Coordinating their times-off proved not as easily accomplished as they'd anticipated. As a travel agent, with a choice of several airlines, Marla managed to list herself for "space available" on a fairly open flight with United. Naomi and Reba, both reservation agents but for different airlines, booked themselves on standby with their respective employers. They scheduled their arrival in Boston within an hour of one another. Marla would arrive first.

Thank goodness for cell phones, Marla thought, or she might still be sitting in the Boston airport, waiting for her friends. Deplaning at United Airlines D Gate, she scurried toward Delta's terminal to meet Naomi. A tinkling summons from her cell phone halted her self-imposed marathon. It was Reba, stranded in Minneapolis after being bumped from her connecting flight.

"The rest of today's flights look pretty full," she grumbled. "I don't see me getting out of here until tomorrow, at the earliest."

Marla quickly punched in Naomi's number, hoping her friend could accept the call "on-plane." What a relief to hear her voice.

"Naomi," Marla wailed into her cell phone. "We have a problem. Reba is stranded in Minneapolis."

"Tell me about it," was Naomi's terse response. "I'm stuck here in Seattle. The fog rolled in right after your plane took off. All flights have been cancelled, which means there probably won't be space available until tomorrow . . . if I'm lucky."

To Marla, it seemed her only option would be to wait in a hotel room until her companions caught flights into Boston.

"There's no point in spending money on a hotel." Naomi was already anticipating her friend's rationale. "Pick up the car at Hertz and go out to the cottage. It's not that far. Reba and I will call when we get in and you can come pick us up." She hesitated. "That is, if you think you can find Ed's place."

Marla knew her friend was making reference to her notoriety for being directionally disadvantaged. "I can find it," Marla retorted defensively. "Just give me directions I can follow."

Finally satisfied her carefully charted instructions were transferred onto paper, Naomi concluded with - "The key is under the mat. We'll call you tomorrow."

Once Marla conquered the long lines and endless questions at Ground Transportation, it became only a matter of getting out of Boston, a challenge she met with surprising ease. Naomi's verbal map proved as easily mastered; off-ramps to the highway north clearly marked. At first, Marla was quite pleased with herself, but as she advanced farther into the rural area, her smugness began to wane. Not only were faded street signs barely readable, sometimes they didn't exist at all. After a frustrating series of wrong turns, Marla surrendered to the humiliation of frequent stops asking for directions. Unfortunately, they often proved to be of the "turn right just past Murphy's barn" variety.

It was late afternoon when, just outside the so described "quaint little New England fishing village," Marla finally located the dirt road that, according to Naomi's directions, would lead to her brother's cottage. To Marla's dismay, the road extended only part way to a solitary cabin perched on the edge of a bluff; the final five hundred feet uphill could only be navigated on foot. Thankful for the sturdy little wheels on her luggage, she struggled up the path, her "now-worldly-goods" bumping along behind her.

Quite winded when, at long last, she reached the little covered porch, Marla paused to catch her breath, then stooped to the mat to retrieve the hidden key. Carefully lifting the sand-encrusted square of straw, she let it drop with a thud. *Oh, swell*, she fumed inwardly. *No key*! Snatching the worn doorknob, she jiggled it in angry frustration. To her surprise, the door offered no resistance. It was not locked.

One hesitant step across the threshold put her in the center of what obviously served as the cabin's "great room"; cook stove, couch, kitchen table and chairs sharing the same limited space. A few more short steps covered the distance to the window. Pulling back the drapes, Marla caught her breath at the sight of the exposed expanse of sandy beach and undulating surface of Cape Cod Bay greeting her. Mesmerized, she watched as the sun slowly melted into glistening waters, its colors spreading like spilled paint across the Bay. For a moment, the hostility festering inside her disappeared.

Unfortunately, reality re-instated itself as she turned back to complete her inspection of their rustic vacation accommodations. Two doors stood at the far end of the room. Crossing the bare wood floor, Marla pushed open the door to a bedroom, its one double bed leaving no doubt but that one of their threesome would be sleeping on the couch. The second doorway led to a tiny, hopelessly inadequate, bathroom, exposed studs suggesting its completion still in progress.

A scowl dug into Marla's forehead as her gaze slid across the austerity of their vacation lodgings. "Two weeks," she muttered. "Two glorious weeks. That might be just a tad longer than I can handle."

Having little other option until her friends arrived, Marla set about unpacking. That chore quickly dispatched, she turned back into the cabin's unappealing great room. A second perusal of the cramped quarters revealed an assortment of driftwood neatly stacked in a box beside the stove. With the discovery came the unwelcome realization, this would undoubtedly prove to be the sole source of heat, both for warmth against the night air as well as for cooking their meals. For tonight, she decided, the apple she'd tucked in her purse would satisfy what little appetite she had. Unable, however, to ignore the chilling evening dampness crowding into the room, she reluctantly set about the unfamiliar task of building a fire.

After several disheartening attempts, Marla managed to encourage a tiny yellow flame beneath the dried beach wood. Retrieving her apple and her paperback edition of *Runaway to Tahiti*, she switched on the lamp and curled up on the couch.

Rodg and Helen, the adventurous protagonists in her chosen novel, were just securing the lines of the Sea Witch to the dock at Westport, when an unfamiliar sound from outside the cabin intruded upon her concentration. Marla glanced over her shoulder, peering through the opaque window framed by the still open drapes. The ocean had swallowed the light of day but in the fading twilight, she saw . . .. Her heart stumbled; her constricted throat refused passage to the tart fruit she held in her mouth. A man's figure briefly outlined itself against the pale sky, then was gone, disappearing into the murky shadows of the approaching night. Marla's eyes probed the deepening darkness. Had she imagined it, or was someone there, just outside her window, watching?

CHAPTER TWO

Having drawn the blinds and secured the cabin door, Marla huddled on the couch, wrapped in her own embrace as she struggled to rationalize her fears into submission. It could have just been a late evening stroller, passing outside the window, she reasoned. A pragmatic subconscious refused to be pacified, reminding her this cabin sat on the edge of a bluff. Merely her imagination, then? The shadowy figure etched upon her mind's eye would not be so easily erased. It had been a long, difficult day. She knew she was over-reacting, knew there was a plausible explanation. Meanwhile, she was scared out of her wits.

Marla wasn't sure how long she cowered there on the sagging settee, leaving its haven only to feed the sputtering fire, before she noticed the box beside the stove, its once-ample supply of wood having dwindled away to nearly nothing.

"This is foolish," she scolded herself. "I'm a grown woman. There is nothing to fear. The windows are closed, the door is locked . . . ."

Her breath struggled for passage through the unexpected constriction of her throat. *Wait! The key . . . the key that was supposed to be under the mat . . . if she didn't have it, who did?* The diminishing stack of wood suddenly lost its importance. Dragging a chair from its place at the table, Marla wedged it firmly beneath the black metal of the doorknob. Satisfied the safety of her fortress was adequately secured, she reached for the switch on the floor lamp, firmly twisting it off, then, as sudden darkness enveloped her, twisting it back on.

"Just in case I need a glass of water during the night," she explained to the empty room.

Having made certain the bedroom window was securely fastened

Marla warily contemplated the questionable comfort of the room's sagging four-poster bed. Discarding her plan of slipping into her nightclothes and crawling between its sheets, she removed her shoes and lay down atop the chenille spread, covering herself with the wool blanket draped at the foot of the bed. For a long while, she lay staring, dry-eyed, into the darkness, certain sleep would elude her this night. But the stress of the day soon caught up with her and she dozed off.

Groggily groping her way through semi-awareness, Marla struggled to identify the sound awakening her, fumbled to recognize unfamiliar surroundings. Her sleep-blurred vision focused upon the doorway and the vague figure silhouetted against the dim light from the great room. For a moment, she was a frightened child again, fearful of the intimidating darkness. Her father would curl up beside her, comfort her until she fell back asleep. She closed her eyes, basking in the warm comfort of security.

A harsh sound of metal grating against metal shattered the euphoric bubble of her fantasy. Jolted back into merciless reality, she felt her limbs grow rigid with terror. She was no longer that little girl; the figure in the doorway was not her father. She peered fearfully into the darkness. A scream clawed at the back of her throat, but before it could escape the prison of her clenched jaws, she realized the intruder was gone. With trembling fingers, Marla clutched the blanket to her chin, her ears straining for a sound from the next room. There was only silence.

Carefully, Marla slid her legs across the chenille cover, lowering her feet to the cold wood floor. Her hand, searching across the uncarpeted surface for a weapon with which to fell her enemy, closed about the flimsy wire of a clothes hanger. Thus armed, she cautiously edged her way to the door, peering into the room beyond.

Her anxious gaze, probing dark corners for some sign of her nemesis, paused upon the bathroom's closed portal. Brandishing the inadequate weapon above her head, she crept across the room, scarcely aware of rough, splintered flooring tearing at her nylon-clad feet. Dragging a gulp of courage into her lungs, she burst into the little chamber only to find it empty.

On unsteady legs she turned back into the main room, relieved her would-be assailant was gone. But how, she panicked, did he get into the cabin? Her eyes darted to the cabin door. An icy chill slithered along her spine. The chair remained wedged in the same position she'd left it the night before. A quick inspection of its lock, then the still fastened windows, revealed nothing disturbed. Did she imagine it all? Marla pressed her hands to her throbbing temples. What was happening to her? Was she losing her mind?

Sleep ceased to be an option. Wrapping herself in the blanket she dragged from the bedroom, Marla curled up on the couch where she would spend the rest of the night keeping a watchful eye on the doorway. Her Puckish thoughts taunted her with the image of a pleasantly warm airport terminal where she imagined her friends comfortably awaiting "space available." As she swiped the corner of the blanket across the moisture gathering at the end of her cold nose, Marla's vengeful speculations turned toward the next anticipated conversation with Naomi regarding brother Ed's "adorable" Cape Cod cottage.

❋   ❋   ❋

The first timid light of dawn was nudging the hopsack draperies when Marla awoke. Amazed she had slept at all she unraveled herself from her woolen cocoon and pulled aside the window coverings. Fears of the night before dissolved as her gaze swept across an inviting expanse of sand stretching out to meet the glistening waters of the bay. Her heart quickened with anticipation of a stroll along the beach.

A glance at the inadequacy of the travel clothes she still wore, rumpled from a restless night's sleep, sent Marla scurrying into the bedroom where a quick search of her luggage produced a pair of jeans and a turtleneck sweater. Foraging further, she pulled forth a pair of walking shoes, stuffing her feet into their cold, uncompromising stiffness. Shrugging into her parka, she stopped only long enough to snatch her purse from the couch before stepping out into the brisk New England morning.

Greedily filling her lungs with the pungent ocean air, Marla turned her eager steps toward the bay and the invitation of its beach. A moment later, she stood at the edge of the bluff, staring morosely down the steep embankment to the sandy stretch below, her excited anticipation of a moment ago a shriveled lump of bitter disappointment. The cabin's inaccessibility from the ocean's shore, so reassuring the night before, now denied her the dearest of her pleasures. With a sigh of annoyance, she plopped down upon the brittle mesa grass. Another glitch, she fumed, in this disaster of a vacation.

Marla gazed wistfully to where, further down the beach another early riser sauntered through the nebulous morning mist, his presence offering momentary comfort. A sudden chilling fog of loneliness settled over her. Maybe, when Naomi and Reba get here, she thought, things won't seem so dismal. At this time next year, she fantasized they'd look back and laugh about the vacation gone sour. Sharing made it an adventure, alone . . ..

Plowing through her purse, Marla located her cell phone. Flipping open its cover, she punched in the numbers meant to connect her with Naomi. Irritating static scratched at her ear. Impatiently, she substituted Reba's code, but the same gravelly sound greeted her. With the realization she was out of range came the disturbing thought, if she couldn't reach them, her friends wouldn't be able to contact her when they arrived in Boston. She'd just have to drive back to the little fishing village where, hopefully, cell phone reception would be better.

Rising quickly to her feet, she turned toward the cabin. By the time her hurried stride brought her to her destination she'd decided, instead, to toss a few necessities into an overnight bag and, if her traveling companions hadn't caught a flight yet, go on into Boston where she could wait for them in the comfort of a hotel room. Pushing open the cabin's weathered door, she was halfway across the great room before she sensed something not quite right with her surroundings. It was a moment of bewilderment before awareness sent prickly gremlins of fear cavorting through the hairs at the back of her neck. Last night, depletion of the wood supply forced her to seek reinforcement from a woolen blanket to ward off the chill and dampness. Yet now, the cabin's interior was pleasantly warm.

An energetic fire crackled inside the little cook stove. For an instant, hysteria threatened as questions of self-doubt tumbled through Marla's mind. Perhaps the embers hadn't been dead; the wood not entirely reduced to ashes. Her eyes darted uneasily about the empty room while anxiety knotted her stomach. Quickly discarding her earlier plan for a necessity-packed overnight bag, within a few frantic moments she'd crammed all her belongings back into her suitcase, and was hurrying out the door.

To Marla, it seemed her wheeled luggage, so burdensome on the way up to the cabin, was now as eager as she to leave this place. Nipping at her heels, it would have passed her had she not kept a firm grip on its handle. After an exhausting struggle to control its impatience, so they might reach the bottom of the pathway at the same time, Marla gratefully lifted the willful case into the trunk of the waiting Hertz rental car. She paused long enough to wipe away the moisture clinging to the car windows before sliding behind the wheel. Inserting it into its slot, she turned the key in the ignition. No sound came from beneath the vehicle's hood. Once again, this time furiously pumping the gas pedal, she twisted the notched bit of metal in its slot; still nothing.

Popping the hood latch, she stomped to the front of the car and lifted the square of metal covering its innards; revealing a collection of parts about which she knew nothing. The engine was intact, that she knew. Everything else was a mystery. She jiggled a few lines, tugged at a few wires. Everything seemed to be in its place. *No, wait.* A frown puckered her forehead. *Those loose hanging wires; shouldn't they be connected to something? Was a part missing?*

Marla slammed the hood shut. Through tears of frustration, she glared down the rutted dirt road and its unappealing option. How far could it be back to that fishing village? She'd taken so many wrong turns coming here it was impossible for her to guess the distance. Reluctantly, her gaze crawled back to the top of the bluff and the little cabin which, by now, had taken on the eerie ambience of *Bates Motel*. Snatching her purse from the front seat, Marla turned toward what she hoped was the direction to the village.

CHAPTER THREE

Her feet hurt! Her legs ached! The warmth Marla welcomed from her early morning wardrobe now threatened to hasten her demise. It helped to remove her parka, wrap its arms about her waist. But as the sun rose higher and the day warmer, the turtleneck sweater took on all the comforts of a hair shirt. How far had she walked, how much further to the village? Was she even going in the right direction? Despair urged her to reconsider, to retrace her steps, when, rounding one last bend in the road, there it was, shimmering in the distance, a cluster of buildings that must surely be the village.

Contemplating the sun's overhead position, along with the painful contractions of her neglected stomach, Marla suspected it must be close to noon. With her destination finally in sight, she decided it might be a good time to try to contact Naomi and Reba. Stumbling to a rock conveniently situated at the road's edge, Marla gratefully lowered herself onto its gritty surface. Digging into the pocket of her parka, she located her cell phone. Selection of Naomi's code produced immediate results. Tears of relief filled Marla's eyes at the familiar sound of her friend's voice.

"Naomi," she croaked.

"Marla!" The responding screech, careening through space, rudely invaded Marla's vulnerable ear. "We've been worried sick about you. We've been trying to reach you all night." The words swarmed from Marla's receiver like angry bees. "Reba and I got in late. When we couldn't reach you, we had to take a taxi. We've been calling and calling. Where have you been?"

Marla elbowed her way into a momentary pause in the tirade.

"Where do you think I've been?" she snapped. "I've been at your brother's cabin."

Dead air hovered between them. Then, "Marla, Reba and I are at Ed's cabin."

"Oh, lordy." Marla's hand dropped weakly into her lap as, following the sudden gush of comprehension, a tsunami of humiliation washed over her.

"Look," Naomi's voice commanded from atop Marla's jean-clad knee. "If I give you directions again, do you think you could . . ."

Marla pressed the phone back to her ear. "I can't," she interrupted.

"Now, Marla, of course you can."

Marla chose to ignore the exasperation she heard in her friend's voice. "The car doesn't work," she confessed, her own voice a helpless monotone.

"What do you mean, the car doesn't work? Why haven't you called a mechanic? Well, never mind. Tell me where you are, and I'll have Phil at the service station come check the car."

"I'm sitting on a rock, outside of what I hope is the village. The car is…well, now I have no idea where the car is."

"Just stay where you are, Marla. I'll send Phil out to pick you up."

Good, Marla thought, snapping the phone cover shut, b*ecause I have no intention of moving my aching, miserable body from this spot.*

Less than thirty minutes later, Marla was climbing into the cab of a pickup, its driver having identified himself as "Phil from the service station". One look at her disheveled appearance seemed to clue him as to his passenger's state of mind.

"I 'spect first off you'll be wantin' to join yoah friends at Ed Balcom's place. Can you tell me wheah you left the cah?"

Marla motioned vaguely in the direction from which she'd just come. "It's parked at the end of some driveway, just below a little cabin, gray I think it is, that sits up on a high bluff.

Phil's head pivoted toward the young woman seated beside him, his eyebrows arched in surprise. "That theah sounds like Jacob's place."

"When you see this Jacob," Marla faltered, cringing at the thought of the man whose privacy she'd usurped the night before, "will you please make my apologies. I had no idea I was trespassing. I thought he was the trespasser."

Phil was silent for a moment. "Somebody was theah?"

"Well … yes."

"Hmm, musta been a beach comber. Jacob ain't been seen in these heah pahts since…" he hesitated. "Theah was that big stohm last Mahch," he finally continued. "Nevah found Jacob, or his boat."

❦   ❦   ❦

Wrapped in a warm robe, a chilled glass of Vouvray in her hand, Marla stared into the comforting flames crackling in the big stone fireplace gracing the living room wall of Ed's cottage. Beside it, a large picture window afforded a view of the evening sunset. French doors opened out onto a slate patio, the sand dunes and beach grass beyond. The mouth-watering odors of a bubbling pot of Dinty Moore's Beef Stew drifted from the kitchen. Phil and his apprentice returned the rental car to Ed's driveway saying it started right up for them.

Marla good-naturedly endured her companions' chiding about the dysfunctional sense of direction which put her in the wrong cabin; her total lack of mechanical knowledge when she referred to the missing part beneath the car's hood. Unwilling to dwell upon her escapade, she'd accepted their rationalization, putting a drifter outside the cabin's window that first evening; him building a fire in the cook stove the following morning when he thought she'd left, perhaps the very man she'd seen strolling the beach.

But Marla was reluctant to share the entire episode with them. She'd not told them of awakening to find a shadowy figure watching her from the doorway of the bedroom, the figure of someone who unexplainably managed to enter the cabin through locked windows and a barricaded door. She knew they'd only attribute it to her overactive imagination. But was it? Marla wasn't so sure.

CHAPTER FOUR

How comforting the sand felt, its gritty warmth massaging the soles of her bare feet. Carefully avoiding an odious garland of drying kelp, Marla moved closer to the water's edge where the firm wet sand was etched with a montage of tiny three pronged prints left by the bevy of sandpipers scurrying ahead of her. Startled sand crabs, sidestepping over the smooth sand, scuttled toward the shelter of nearby rocks. Diminutive waves rushed forward to splash across her toes then, like teasing children, darted back to the sheltering arms of an anxious mother. Graceful gulls swooped overhead, screeching raucous morning greetings. Marla filled her lungs with the ambrosia of salty sea air. Here, in the ultimate perfection of her world, yesterday's trauma seemed far away.

She was glad she decided not to accompany Naomi and Reba on their local tour of inspection; relieved they accepted her excuse of exhaustion from yesterday's forced march. Standing at the edge of the patio, she watched impatiently as her two companions strolled off toward the village. The moment they were out of sight, she hurried back into the cottage, slipped into a pair of shorts and a halter and headed for her favorite retreat, the beach. In the comfort and solace of her surroundings, she was able to re-examine the ordeals of that first day of vacation, grateful for last night's sleep in a secure environment and the soothing wonders it performed upon her ragged nerves.

As it frequently happened when she walked the beach, her thoughts her only companions, Marla soon lost track of time and distance. Momentarily abandoning her unconscious study of the shell-strewn sand, she glanced down the windswept beach, her gaze coming to rest upon a jumbled pile of shipwrecked logs huddled at the base of a rocky bluff. Atop the bluff, perched at its edge, stood a small cabin; an eternal sentinel, its gray weathered siding blending with the early morning sky.

Like an invisible fog rolling in from the sea, blotting out the sun's warmth, a chill swept over Marla. She shuddered, recognizing the dwelling where she'd spent the long, frightful hours two nights before. Unwelcome memories crowded around her; the man outside the window, the shadowy figure in the bedroom doorway, the unexplainable morning fire in the cook stove, the loose wires beneath the car's hood. What she thought she'd left behind as a seemingly bad dream, now loomed ahead to taunt her.

How did she end up here? Surely she couldn't have repeated yesterday's journey in so short a time. Panic threatened to overtake her until logic restored her faltering judgement. The distance along the beach would probably be more direct, shorter than the winding, twisting roadway.

Her first instinct was to turn back the way she'd come, to put as much sandy beach as possible between her and this disturbing specter. But a strange compulsion urged her forward. Marla found herself standing at the base of the cliff, staring up at its sheer insurmountable wall of stone. A tiny seed of uneasiness sprouted within her chest. From where she stood, it would be impossible for anyone to scale that rocky surface worn smooth by windblown sand and sea. Just as she was certain someone had been outside the cabin's window that night, she was now more certain than ever it could not have been a casual beachcomber.

🍁　　🍁　　🍁

Her stroll on the beach ceased to be a leisurely one, her main intent now being to reach their vacation cottage before Naomi and Reba returned from the village. Marla wanted to avoid having to explain her reason for taking the car, her reason for driving back to the cabin on the bluff. Because that is exactly what she intended to do, what she had to do now, today, before the voracious doubts nibbling at her rationale completely devoured her sanity. For, whether a curse or a blessing, hers was an insatiable curiosity, which, once challenged, would give her no rest until satisfied.

Time-wise, the journey back along the beach proved a shorter one. Marla forced herself to slow her galloping gait as she neared their temporary-home-for-the-next-two weeks, fought to control her labored breathing as she carefully slid open the patio doors. Relieved, she slowly released the air she'd held trapped in her lungs. All appeared quiet with no sign of her two companions.

Hastily shoving her sand-covered feet into a pair of sandals, Marla snatched the car keys from their hook. She was about to slip out the back door when she noticed the message pad stationed upon the wall. Reminded she should probably reassure her friends the car hadn't been stolen, she eased her conscience with a short scribbled note "Back soon" before continuing on her way.

Anxiety and lack of faith in her directional prowess tightened Marla's hands upon the steering wheel as she guided the car along the route she'd followed two days earlier. Hazily recalled landmarks assisted her recalcitrant memory, urging her along a vaguely familiar route into a poorly marked turnoff and onto the dusty road leading to the little gray cabin atop the bluff. Parking where the roadway ended at the bottom of the steep trail leading to the cabin, Marla stepped from the car, pausing for a moment to stare up at her nemesis, crouching above her like a hungry predator. Then, with a resolve she did not feel she forced her reluctant feet onto the pathway.

At the end of the sandy trail, she hesitated at the edge of the tiny plateau. Now, standing closer to the cabin, Marla decided it lost some of its sinister look; exuded, instead, an aura of pathos; a loneliness. She glanced about at the desolate surroundings but saw no visible signs of life.

Deliberately, she made her way to the ocean side of the little building where an embankment dropped sharply to the sandy beach below. A capricious breeze, dancing among the slender beach grasses, abandoned its swaying partner to tangle in the young woman's hair, whipping the long auburn strands across her eyes and into the corners of her mouth. Dragging the tossing maelstrom from her face, Marla focused her attention upon the purpose of her visit. Carefully circling the building, then circling it again, she investigated every windswept foot of the isolated mesa until her curiosity had finally been satisfied.

The only possible access to this site was by way of the path she'd just ascended: the only entry to the cabin, its one door.

Marla hesitated before the weathered panel. Tentatively, she reached out, closing her fingers about the black metal knob. As before, it turned easily and, with little encouragement, the door swung inward. She peered into the familiar dimness inside, then cautiously stepped across the threshold.

The room appeared no different than the first time she'd seen it: cold, uninviting. The coarse, hopsack draperies were slightly open, letting light from the mid-morning sun poke inquisitive fingers into murky corners. Marla found herself tiptoeing as she crossed the bare wood floor to peek through the open door of the bedroom. Her heart skipped a beat as she recognized the wool blanket she'd left in a disheveled heap on the couch, now neatly folded and returned to its place at the foot of the bed. An anxious check of the bathroom reassured her she was alone in the cabin. It was as she'd first found it - but not as she'd left it.

There was no fire in the stove to warm the room. Yet the once-empty box beside the stove now embraced a bountiful supply of dry driftwood, as if in preparedness. A sudden uneasiness prickled the back of Marla's neck sending her scurrying back out into the welcome brightness of the day. Quickly closing the door, she turned her back upon this place of mystery and foreboding and hastened down the pathway to her waiting car.

Sliding behind the wheel, Marla inserted the key into the ignition. For a moment her heart fluttered to the back of her throat, then relief surged through her at the comforting sound of the engine growling into life. Releasing the brake, Marla shifted gears, casting one last farewell glance toward the forlorn little structure above her, its silvery gray weathered shingles, its sea of beach grass bending to the whim of a willful ocean breeze.

Then she saw him, the tall, lanky figure of a man, standing at the top of the pathway. Even with the distance existing between them Marla could make out the fisherman's cap pulled low over his eyes, his hands thrust into the pockets of a foul-weather jacket. Fear jammed her foot onto the gas pedal sending her Hertz rental hurtling down the dusty road. Framed in the rear view mirror, the ominous figure at the top of the bluff silently watched her departure.

CHAPTER FIVE

It would have been too much to hope Naomi and Reba would still be away. The cottage door, open to the cool afternoon breeze, alerted Marla to her friends' presence as she careened into the driveway. Actually, she was relieved to find them there. She felt in dire need of moral support at that moment albeit it would undoubtedly be critical in nature. Her fingers fumbled with the ignition key and Marla realized how badly her hands were shaking. She struggled to steady her nerves, organize her thoughts, before facing her two companions.

Did she want them to know she'd gone back to the deserted cabin? What if she told them about the man she'd seen on the pathway? Would they believe her or think she was "losing it?" Just another interloper, they'd rationalize, as she had been. At best, she knew she'd receive a lecture on this repeat of her trespassing offense.

It was Naomi who interrupted Marla's moment of indecisive introspection. She stood in the doorway, her expression vacillating from concern to annoyance.

Hoping to corral her errant courage, Marla took a deep breath and opened the car door. "Hi, Naomi," she chirped innocently. "I didn't expect you back this soon so I decided to take a little drive." She decided she wasn't ready to share her morning's experience. "You know, sort of get acquainted with the area," she suggested.

Any hope an airy greeting might divert a confrontation disappeared as a frown settled itself between Naomi's brows. "You should have waited for Reba and me," she scolded. "We would have gone with you." Though unspoken, both knew Naomi's concern stemmed from Marla's propensity for getting lost.

"No problem." Marla offered a reassuring smile. "At least I found my way home, that's a plus, huh?"

"Well, there's something to be said for that, I suppose." Naomi's forced a tight smile. "So, where did you go?"

"Oh, no place in particular," Marla shrugged "Just checking out the lay of the land."

Wariness deepened Naomi's frown. The longevity of their friendship gave her an insight into Marla's thinking processes, familiarized her with the tenacity of a frequently imprudent curiosity.

By the same measure, Marla, aware of the doubts aroused by her evasive response, could almost read her friend's thoughts, hear the suspicions forming in her mind. She cringed knowing the next inevitable question would be one she wasn't ready to answer.

"Hey, Marla." Reba's cherubic face appeared over Naomi's shoulder. "Where've you been? We've been worried about you." Not waiting for a response, which was typically Reba, she bubbled on, eager to share her own day. "You missed a great outing. You should have gone with us. You've just got to go with us tomorrow. You'll love this little village."

"Sounds like a great idea to me," Marla quickly agreed, welcoming this diversion from Naomi's probing. "I'll be up and ready to go when you are. Meanwhile, what's for lunch? I'm starved."

❦   ❦   ❦

True to her promise, Marla was up and dressed long before Reba and Naomi tumbled sleepily from their beds. By the time they finished their toiletries, Marla had downed two cups of very strong coffee. Thus fortified, she felt prepared to put the past two days behind her and looked forward to spending a day with her friends. Reba's exuberant chatter was constant, fed by her eagerness to share the discoveries of the day before. Naomi's demeanor, however, was more reserved, almost distant. The little frown plucking at her forehead suggested she still struggled with yesterday's doubts and unanswered questions. An uneasy tension hovered between the three as they set off on their invasion of the fishing village.

The quaint little community turned out to be all Reba professed and, like her, Marla found herself captivated by the charm of its simplicity. Tiny shops, resisting the commercial dilution of tourist influence, were a delight. Catering only to the needs of local clientele, they afforded an opportunity to experience the true flavor of a very different way of life from the one to which the young Seattlites were accustomed.

To the delight of the three young travelers, their early morning arrival at the Village Square coincided unexpectedly with that of several local fishermen. Yards of fishing nets lay spread across the cobblestones. Smooth-faced or bewhiskered, their sun-tanned faces, lined by wind and weather, the mariners seemed to share a sort of sameness, an agelessness, as they bent to the task of mending their nets. Except for one.

Slouched casually against the low wall circumventing the square, one hip perched upon the sun-bleached stones, the olive-skinned, clean-shaven young fisherman stood apart from the others. Broad, muscular shoulders, ill-concealed beneath a thin, dingy-gray tee shirt, narrow hips girded by worn but snug-fitting jeans, his strong, callused hands deftly guided a twine-threaded needle through the coarse webbing of damaged mesh. To the appreciative eye of his female observers, he absolutely oozed an aura of raw masculinity.

Marla glanced toward Reba and seeing they shared the same point of interest, arched her eyebrows. As if anticipating her friend's reaction, Reba grinned, dimples parenthesizing her impish smile.

"Wow," she mouthed, eyes twinkling.

"All right, you two," an ever-serious Naomi hissed. "Behave yourselves."

An irrepressible giggle escaped from behind the fingers Reba pressed to her lips. The dark-haired "Adonis" shifted his attention from the nets to where his admirers stood on the opposite side of the square. A smile slashed a white crescent across his bronzed face as he dropped one eyelid in a slow, deliberate wink.

Each with an elbow cradled in Naomi's grip, Reba and Marla were unceremoniously herded across the street and into the protective doorway of a bookstore. Hands on hips, Naomi turned to face her errant companions.

"Honestly! You two are just awful," she scolded.

Her feigned display of indignity was betrayed by the traitorous smile toying with the corner of her mouth. In the next moment, all three of them were leaning weakly against the building, wiping tears of laughter from their cheeks. The tension was broken. Marla suppressed a sigh of relief. Once again they were just three friends off on a vacation, sharing an adventure.

They spent the day foraging through the treasures of their Cape Cod hide-away. They prowled through tiny nondescript shops, discovered the local chandlery where they puzzled over strange apparatus designed to catch the bigger fish; giggled over their lame attempts to mimic the unfamiliar local vernacular. Noontime found them skeptically contemplating lunch at a small café called Mo's Shanty. Hunger and weariness dictated their decision to disregard its lack of frontage appeal. Once inside, their skepticism only increased.

"What are you going to have?" Reba whispered, scanning the food-stained menu.

"Looks like today's special is something called soft shelled blue crab," Naomi volunteered. "Do you like crab?"

"Well, I know I like dungeness crab, but what's blue crab, and what difference does it make if the shell is soft?"

"There's a blurb on the back of the menu," Marla interrupted. "It says here the blue crab is native to the western Atlantic Ocean." Marla scanned the excerpt for a moment "According to this, while over-harvesting has made the crab less plentiful, apparently the soft shelled version is an even rarer delicacy. It seems it has to be harvested during a limited period of time, just after molting and before the new shell has time to harden."

Naomi wrinkled her nose. "I'm not sure I'm that interested in hearing the evolutionary processes of whatever I'm ordering for lunch," she sniffed.

Reba flipped her menu over to scan the printed offering. "You'll want to hear this, Naomi," she snickered. "This says during courtship, the male crab performs a sort of wild, provocative dance meant to lure the female out of hiding." She was unable to suppress the giggle erupting from her lips. "They call it 'the blue crab boogie'."

"No wonder the females go into hiding," Naomi quipped.

In the end, though somewhat hesitantly, the trio opted to sample the daily special, a plate of tiny, crisply fried, soft-shelled crab, which they consumed with more than a little trepidation.

❦   ❦   ❦

By late afternoon, they'd had a full, but exhausting, day. Marla was tired and her feet hurt. Her thoughts turned longingly to the cottage, coveting its comforts and the promise of a regenerating glass of chilled Vouvray.

"Let's visit the museum before we leave." The enthusiastic suggestion came from Reba with her seemingly boundless energy.

"We can do that tomorrow, Reba," Marla argued, yearning for the suddenly elusive glass of wine. "We don't have to see everything in one day."

"I know you two," Reba persisted. "Naomi will want to flake out on the patio and read; you'll be off to the beach. Come on," she urged. "It won't take that long and you'll be glad you did it."

"She's right, you know," Naomi sighed. "If being glad only means we won't have to listen to her nagging."

The maritime museum was small, boasting of a scanty collection of old boats, a few mementos of early fishing methods along with an exhibit commemorating the local fishermen lost at sea. Wandering aimlessly among the uninspiring trivia, Marla paused before the memorial display, its collection of yellowing photos imprisoned against the wall behind a flyspecked sheet of glass. Her gaze slid listlessly over the faded images, indistinct counterparts captured on low quality film by well-meaning amateurs. Identifying notations had been penciled below each grainy square.

A grizzled seaman glowered from his cocoon of foul-weather gear. "Eric Johnson: Captain of the Marcie D," the caption revealed. "Boat capsized off St. Mary's Reef, storm of '68". In another photo, a smooth-faced, younger version, smiled disarmingly from beneath his sou'wester. "John Alderwood: Crewman aboard the Loretta Lynn. Washed overboard, storm of '77'." Marla's lethargic interest drifted to another sharper, obviously more recent, photograph. Her next breath became a strangled gasp as her constricted throat fought to discourage an unwelcome resurrection of her restless lunch of soft-shelled crab. She glanced quickly toward her companions, hoping they hadn't heard her gurgle of distress, relieved to find them deeply embroiled in a controversy over the questionable merits of the whale harpoon. She turned back to stare at the glossy reproduction preserved beneath the smudged pane of glass.

Hands jammed into the pockets of his foul-weather jacket, a fisherman's cap pulled low onto his forehead, a tall, lanky fisherman stared back at her. It was as if she was seeing his image again; the gaunt figure made ominous by its sudden, unexpected appearance, watching her as she sped away from the little gray cabin. The air inside the museum suddenly became dank, heavy. The rapid staccato of her excited heart pounded in her ears. Numbly, she bent to study the inscription scrawled beneath the apparition. "Jacob Mallory. Captain of the Sea Nymph," it read. "Presumably lost at sea, storm of March '03."

A chill crept into the room, wrapping its arms around her. Marla shivered knowing it was not from the dampness. She tried to close her mind to the rabble of questions filling her mind, goading a curiosity that often undermined good judgement. Yet, she knew her efforts were useless. That relentless curiosity, already aroused, would not be appeased until she found answers - answers that would only be found at a little, gray cabin overlooking the ocean.

CHAPTER SIX

Sleep did not come easily that night. Marla's efforts to wrestle her goose-down pillow into submission failed miserably and she spent long wakeful hours staring into the darkness, listening to the turbulent sounds of the ocean. Agitated waves pummeling the beach, grinding tiny rocks into tinier bits of sand echoed the unrest roiling through her own mind. On the late evening news, the local meteorologist predicted a change in the weather, one that would certainly alter any sight seeing plans for tomorrow and maybe even longer. While Marla suspected foul weather conditions would undoubtedly restrict her friends to the confines of the cottage, she had no intention of letting that happen to her.

As always, Marla eagerly awaited the exhilarating thrill of an ocean storm, the excitement of challenging its buffeting winds, defying the threat of its pompous rain-filled clouds. While she looked forward to the upcoming tempest, she knew this time it would be for reasons other than the usual anticipated stimulus. Marla was counting on the inclement weather to provide her an opportunity to pursue her plan, a plan she'd craftily devised during those final mind-altering hours of sleeplessness.

🍁　　🍁　　🍁

As predicted, a defused dawn heralded the day's arrival. Cranky winds nattered at the windows while dark, foreboding clouds hunkered low in the sky, contemplating their forthcoming blitzkrieg.

"Oh, swell," grumbled Reba glowering into her glass of orange juice. "There goes half our vacation."

"It's only supposed to last a couple of days," countered an ever-rational Naomi. "It'll give us a chance for a breather. Besides, this is typical New England weather. You can pass this experience on to the next vacationer you book to Cape Cod."

"Lucky me." Disappointment sullied the disposition of their usually cheerful fellow traveler. "Oh, well, such is life," she pouted. "You got a good book I can borrow, Naomi?"

Remaining on the outside edge of their good-natured banter, Marla busied herself gathering the clothing she'd need for her upcoming encounter with the elements. She wriggled her feet into the pair of oversized boots she found closeted alongside a hooded, yellow rain slicker. The waterproof cloak, slipped over her parka, satisfied her less-than-exacting interpretation of what constituted foul weather gear. While Naomi and Reba often questioned the wisdom of Marla's actions, they'd learned to accept the "dog with a bone" tenacity of her decisions. So, amid a volley of allusions as to the stability of her sanity, Marla bravely cast off into the onslaught of the New England storm.

It was the storm god at his best. No sooner had Marla stepped outside when an angry wind pounced upon her, tearing at her clothing with invasive claw-like fingers. Whipping away her suddenly inadequate rain hood, it dipped into the violent surf to fling salty scoops of sea spray across her path. Churlish black clouds hovered overhead, ruthlessly pelting her with torrents of tiny ice missiles. Undaunted, Marla embraced the fury of the storm, welcoming the intensity of its awesome display of unconstrained energy. It was as if some latent entity within her struggled for release, eager to be a part of the swirling forces.

Dragging the hood back onto its protective position upon her head, Marla leaned into the force of the wind, squinting to protect her watering eyes from the sand stinging her face, and headed toward the object of her sleuthing. Inwardly, she was quite pleased with the cleverness of her deception: Without arousing suspicion, she'd succeeded in putting the first phase of her plan into action. Now to decide upon the second phase.

Unfortunately, she had no idea what she intended to do once she reached the little gray cabin. She was almost totally convinced there was no possible access from the beach, yet she had to make certain. Pre-dawn cogitation suggested a more practical plan of utilizing the latitude offered by the rental car, but that would necessitate contriving an excuse Naomi would undoubtedly see through. Besides, Marla wasn't entirely sure she was ready to return to that windy mesa just yet. She only knew, somehow, some way, she needed to quiet the babble of questions addling her brain.

It wasn't long before Marla began to wish she'd thought to wear sunglasses. They couldn't make visibility any worse and would at least offer some protection from the sand. Wiping gritty tears from her eyes, she probed the swirling grayness ahead of her. Surely, she must be nearing the cabin by now. Doubt nibbled at her faltering confidence. It seemed she'd come far enough, but it was difficult to tell. With the storm obliterating any landmarks guiding her beach walk two days ago, uncertainty now slowed her steps.

Yanking her thoughts from where they would stray to an envious contemplation of her two companions, comfortably curled before a warm, toasty fire, Marla squinted down the beach, searching for the identifying pile of sun-bleached logs she'd last seen cowering at the base of a rocky bluff. Nothing looked familiar. The winds had grown more frenzied. Overhead, vengeful clouds dumped another deluge of their icy pellets. With increasingly poor visibility distorting her already warped sense of direction, the storm lost its earlier promise of adventure. The fluttering moth of uneasiness soon spread its wings into a full-grown anxiety. There was no longer any doubt in Marla's mind. She was lost.

Looming ahead of her, shadowy forms of twisted driftwood took shape. Her vision blurred, Marla dragged cold-stiffened fingers across her watering eyes. One shadow seemed to have moved . . . was moving . . . toward her. Relief knotted itself in her throat as she realized she was not alone on the beach. *Thank God*, Marla breathed, *there's another storm enthusiast like myself.* The greeting she was about to fling into the wind was swallowed before it could leave her lips. The shadowy figure emerged from the dimness; body bent into the wind, hands encased in the pockets of a foul weather jacket, a seaman's cap pulled low over his eyes.

Lot's wife couldn't have been more afflicted than Marla at that moment as fear seemingly turned her body to stone. She watched in mute terror as the suddenly ominous figure approached.

She stared numbly into the face now close to her own. Peering back from beneath his seaman's cap were the troubled eyes of an old man. A crisp, graying beard covered his weathered cheeks. Marla watched his moving lips, vaguely aware he was speaking to her, but the wind quickly devoured his words leaving only muffled scraps.

"Stohm . . . gettin' fierce . . .ain't safe . . . follah me . . .." With that fragmented command, the apparition turned and was about to disappear into the swirling mists leaving Marla alone again. The thought jolted her from her comatose state and she hastily stumbled after the departing figure of her Good Samaritan.

CHAPTER SEVEN

Naomi struggled to focus her eyes upon the page, urging them across the orderly rows of words only to find, at the end of the line, the need to repeat the arduous journey. Still, any meaning contained within that jumble of letters failed to penetrate the troublesome thoughts barricading concentration; troublesome thoughts of Marla, somewhere out in this terrible storm. More disturbing was the probability that, considering Marla's directional dysfunction, she was, at this moment, even lost. Naomi glanced uneasily toward the window where a vengeful wind vented its fury against the fragile pane. Her emotions vacillated between concern, frustration, and, yes, even anger: especially anger after discovering Marla's cell phone lying abandoned atop the coverlet of her bed.

In a gesture of irritation, Naomi dragged her slender, manicured fingers through the frosted strands of her bobbed hair. In the years they'd know one another, sharing a friendship as well as vacations, she'd learned to accommodate, if not approve of, Marla's unpredictability: her inability to resist the excitement of a challenge. While Naomi was willing to accept today's storm as an obvious enticement, it certainly did not excuse Marla's irresponsibility. To go off into the unknown perils of an Atlantic coast storm without some means of communication was, in Naomi's opinion, inexcusable.

Shifting her attention, Naomi peered over the top of her book to where Reba, curled up upon the couch, leafed listlessly through the pages of a maritime magazine she'd plucked from the bookshelf. The frequency with which Reba's eyes darted toward the patio, where rivers of rainwater flooded down the outside of the glass doors, betrayed an anxiety which, until now, Naomi had not realized they shared.

Naomi felt a sudden surge of compassion for this younger member of their threesome who'd only recently joined her and Marla in their travels. Recalling her emotions at the time, Naomi revisited her reluctance to include this friend of Marla's in their plans. Over the years, she and Marla managed to establish a comfortable travel arrangement: learned to accommodate one another's diversified interests. Where two were compatible, a third might create conflict. Her misgivings intensified when exposed to Reba's impulsive nature, her seemingly imprudent attraction to the opposite sex.

Time, however, softened Naomi's criticism of their younger companion, she'd come to accept Reba's impulsiveness as a refreshing enthusiasm for adventure, learned to tolerate her naive flirtations as harmless diversions. They formed a strange alliance, Naomi concluded: she with her own fixation on regional culture, Reba's fascination with the local populace, and Marla with her compulsive need to pry beneath the cover of tourist oriented facades. It never really bothered her before, Naomi realized, this Sherlock Holmes fetish of Marla's. But, somehow, this time was different. She wondered if this trip to Cape Cod was such a good idea after all. Perhaps they should alter the perimeters of their vacationing . . . maybe take in the sights of Boston.

"Where is she?"

Reba's abrupt exclamation jolted Naomi from her speculations as her frustrated companion flung her magazine to the floor and rose impatiently from the couch.

"Why isn't she back yet?"

"I'm sure she's okay," Naomi offered an assurance she did not feel. "You know how Marla loves an ocean storm. She's probably having the time of her life."

"You know that's not true." Reba's retort pierced the air with its anxiety. "Marla wouldn't be so foolish as to challenge a storm this bad, unless she was lost . . . or maybe hurt." Reba whirled to face her friend. "How can you just sit there?" she demanded, her voice verging on hysteria. "We should be out looking for her."

"That doesn't make sense, Reba," Naomi scolded softly. "Of course I'm worried, just as you are. But having three of us lost in a storm certainly wouldn't help matters. If she isn't back soon, we'll try calling the police, or maybe even the Coast Guard."

"I'm not waiting," Reba snapped. "I'm calling them now."

Naomi felt a renewed surge of anger toward Marla and the thoughtlessness creating this disharmony. Why, indeed, had she insisted on going out in this storm? What on earth was going on with her? What was the obsession driving her? Naomi could hear Reba's voice coming from the kitchen, the angry frustration being hurled toward someone at the other end of the line, then the sharp click as the receiver was slammed unceremoniously into its cradle.

"They're all busy monitoring aid calls from sea vessels." Her anger depleted, Reba leaned dejectedly against the doorjamb, her eyes filling with tears, her voice ragged with despair. "They can't spare the men for a land search party. They'll send a crew out when the storm has passed."

Naomi glanced nervously toward the terrace where an angry wind assaulted the glass panels with icy pellets of rain. She tried not to think of Marla out in this turbulence, channeling her thoughts instead, toward the more positive aspect of the storm's end and her friend's safe return. Then they would most definitely discuss that trip to Boston.

CHAPTER EIGHT

Marla wrapped her cold fingers around the ceramic mug, coveting the warmth within. No less shamelessly, she hovered close to the little iron pot-bellied stove, soaking up the heat emanating from its black metal sides. Her rain gear, discarded but a few moments before, hung dripping from a hook by the door. She stared into the steaming vessel of liquid held between her hands, her thoughts of self-recrimination as dark as the brew it held. What on earth was wrong with her, she agonized? Whatever possessed her to venture into a near-hurricane pursuing some wild obsession rendering her so paranoid, she all but freaked out at the sight of anyone in a fisherman's cap? She could just imagine the scolding she was sure to receive from Naomi, and probably Reba, too.

Oh lordy! The sudden image of her two friends burst in upon her self-condemnation. *Naomi and Reba! They must be worried sick.* She needed to call them, let them know she was safe. Reluctantly, she released the stiffened fingers of one hand from their arc of warmth and slid them into the pocket of her jeans. The jarring discovery of its emptiness and the ensuing explosion of sudden recall, collided. Her cell phone! Mentally, she visualized that vital medium of communication lying atop the coverlet of her bed where she'd tossed it that morning, deeming it unnecessary baggage on a beach walk.

She glanced up as her bewhiskered rescuer placed a fresh-made pot of coffee atop the little stove. By the remotest of possibilities, she wondered, would he have a telephone? Marla noticed he, too, had removed his rain gear and along with it, the ogre image she'd bestowed upon him.

The beard sheathing his square jaw ascended into the shaggy crown of gray hair which covered his head, then crept down beneath the collar of his blue denim shirt, creating, Marla concluded, an uncanny likeness to Hemingway's *Old Man of the Sea*. Arbitrarily disregarding the fact she was in the same room, and obviously not hard of hearing, this Spencer Tracy prototype was quite audibly muttering about not-so-bright tourists who showed no sense when it came to New England weather. Marla decided it might be best to postpone her quest for a telephone until later.

Her laconic rescuer turned toward her, a scowl upon his face. "This heah's a bad stohm. Nobody with a licka' sense orter be out in it 'less he's got a good reason."

Marla swallowed an impulse to question his reasons for being out in the storm.

Bushy gray brows dipped above a pair of startling blue eyes. "You gotta good reason?"

Marla felt her face redden. "I . . . I was looking for . . . " She hesitated. Those piercing eyes suggested no tolerance for anything other than the truth. "Jacob's cabin," she confessed. "I was headed for Jacob Mallory's cabin."

Those bushy eyebrows leaped toward the old man's hairline. "You know Jacob?"

"Well . . . no, no I don't." Marla could see her stammered confession displeased her interrogator.

"Humph, you passed Jacob's place a long ways back." Those brows returned to hover above narrowed eyes. "He ain't theah, you know."

"Yes, I know, or so I've been told, but ---"

"What business you got at Jacob's cabin, anyway?"

Marla decided the best way to untie this Gordian knot was to tell the whole story. So, while the gnarly fisherman listened, squinting through eyes clouded with suspicion, Marla tried explaining how she'd gotten lost, how she unwittingly spent the first night of her vacation in Jacob's cabin. She hesitated, not sure she if wished to confide in this stranger to the extent of telling him about the man she'd seen there, twice.

The old man seated in the timeworn wooden chair opposite Marla remained silent during her confession. Now, he leaned forward, elbows on his knees, peering at her from those penetrating eyes. "So why you goin' back theah today?"

"There was a man there," Marla heard herself admitting. "I guess I need to know who he was, what he was doing there."

The old man, leaning back in his chair, tugged at the gray bristles of his beard. Marla had the feeling he was trying to decide if she was telling him the truth.

"Twasn't nobody." She was startled by the gruffness of his voice. "Twasn't nobody at all, just some beach combah."

Marla felt herself bristle at his rebuff. "It couldn't have been a beach comber," She insisted. "There's no way to reach that cabin from the beach." Her retort came more sharply than she intended. Fingers steepled beneath his whiskered chin, her frowning host quietly contemplated this sudden outburst. Marla imprisoned her lower lip between her teeth, realizing she'd revealed more than she planned.

The old man folded his hands in his lap, but it was a moment before he spoke. "Folks are mighty private about what goes on 'round heah." Although his voice had lost its gruffness, its sternness warned Marla she was being reprimanded. "Most don't take kindly to meddlin'." He grew silent and somehow, Marla knew it would be better if she remained the same. After a moment, he added, "Them'd be Jacob's feelin's, too."

There was another pause while again she waited for him to speak. When he did so, his gruffness had returned. "It'd be best if you just go back to wheah you came from. Don't go messin' in what's none of yoah business."

The silence settling between them grew long. Marla suspected the old man had said all he intended to say while she, on the other hand, struggled to control the riot of questions his admonition provoked. Was it really a fetish for privacy motivating his warning, a tiny whisper of doubt persisted? Or did he harbor a secret he was afraid she'd discover? He'd spoken of Jacob almost as if he were still alive. Yet the exhibit at the museum labeled him lost at sea. *But wait.* Something stirred in Marla's memory. Didn't the caption beneath his photo list him as "presumably" lost at sea?

Another irritating aggravation; why did everyone keep referring to the man she'd seen outside the cabin as a beachcomber when it was physically impossible for anyone to have scaled the sheer rock of that bluff? Marla could no longer control the riptide of her curiosity.

"I don't mean to intrude upon anyone's privacy," she apologized. "But it just seems strange that . . ."

Her inquisition, barely begun, came to a graceless ending as the old man rose abruptly to his feet. "Looks like the stohm's lettin' up," he announced. "We better be gettin' you back to the village."

The limited view afforded by the tiny window above the linoleum-covered kitchen counter suggested he was right. The persistent rain that earlier flailed against the discolored glass now beat a gentle tattoo upon the shingled roof while a once belligerent wind arbitrarily abandoned its ruthless attack upon the little clapboard shack. Removing any possible doubt the conversation being at an end, "Spencer Tracy" was shrugging into his foul weather gear. Marla had little choice but to do the same.

Obviously, the old seaman planned to accompany her on her journey homeward and while she appreciated the gallantry, Marla rather suspected his decision had more to do with the prevention of any impulsive stopover at the little gray cabin.

CHAPTER NINE

Marla stared, unseeing, at the ceiling of knotty pine creating a canopy over her bed, listening to the silence of early morning. The storm passed during the night giving way to the soggy corpulence of fog now pressing against the cottage window. Marla let her thoughts drift back to the trauma of the day before and the frightening intensity of what she'd considered would be just another stormy day on the beach.

As anticipated, Marla's companions, once assured of her safety, delivered a stern scolding along with a non-negotiable ultimatum. Dutifully contrite, Marla promised if all efforts to curtail her adventurous nature should fail, she would at least always carry her cell phone with her. There was no denying her friends were entirely justified in their anxiety. She would have been at the unforgiving mercy of yesterday's storm if not for the old fisherman.

The memory of her fortunate encounter with that "ancient mariner" proved easily revived. However a mental replay of their conversation only served to stir up a Pandora's box of annoying inconsistencies and doubts for Marla. She knew she should follow the old seaman's advice, forget what did not concern her, simply enjoy her vacation and go home. But she also knew that wasn't likely to happen. The mystery surrounding the gray cabin had become an obsession; one Marla could not relinquish until she resolved the disturbing incongruities even now invading her quiet morning time.

Marla was quite certain the oppressiveness of the gray day would keep her friends' noses buried in their books for a few hours. But once the sun managed to burn its way through the nebulous mists, she knew she'd be expected to join in the sightseeing plans for the day. She welcomed the restricting, though less threatening, weather conditions as an opportunity for an early morning beach walk and perhaps another chance to appease the ravenous appetite of her ever-growing curiosity.

Emerging from her bedroom, she discovered Naomi curled up on the couch deeply engrossed in her book, a glass of orange juice on the table beside her.

"Good morning," Marla offered, wriggling her arms into the sleeves of her parka. "Where's Reba?"

"She's still in bed." A frown skittered across Naomi's forehead as she lowered the book to her lap. "You're not going out in this mess, are you?"

"Hey, no problem, Naomi," To fortify her reassurance, Marla raised the hand clutching her cell phone. "I won't go far. I'll be back soon."

"I thought the three of us might go into the village once this burns off." A poorly concealed displeasure shadowed Naomi's suggestion.

"Not to worry, I'll be back by then." Hoping to escape any further verbalization of her friend's disapproval, Marla turned toward the door only to have guilt stay her hand upon the knob. Naomi's concern was certainly well founded, her conscience reminded her. With her incurable case of directional dysfunction, Marla had to admit her chances of not getting lost in the prevailing foggy conditions were almost non-existent. Did she really want to cause her friends any further distress? After all, she reminded herself, this is supposed to be a fun-filled vacation. With a sigh of resignation, Marla reluctantly dropped her cell phone onto the kitchen counter and let the parka slip from her shoulders.

"You're probably right," she relented. "It is pretty thick out there. What the heck, I can always take my walk later."

It was only ten o'clock when a fastidious mid-morning sun swept away the last residue of murky fog. Over the camaraderie of a leisurely breakfast the three companions discussed plans for their day in the village.

"We could stop by the Village Square," Reba suggested. "The fishermen might be mending nets again today. I really think that's an interesting process to watch."

All too familiar with Reba's flirtatious disposition, Marla suspected the proposal was motivated by the hope of another possible encounter with the dark-haired "Adonis" of two mornings ago.

Naomi, also aware of their companion's coquettish inclinations, was quick to intervene. "There's that charming little book store I've been wanting to visit," she suggested. "We could swing by the Square on our way there."

Comfortably convinced Reba's anticipated adventure would prove quite harmless with Naomi at her side, Marla felt free to voice her dissention. "I'm really not interested in fishnets or antique books," she ventured. "I was hoping to visit the museum. There's some fascinating historical background information I'd like to check out." What she did not share with her friends was the hope of unearthing more information about the ambiguous Jacob Mallory. "Why don't you two go on to the Village Square and the book store. We can meet later at Mo's Shanty for lunch."

A compromise was reached; the morning would be spent with each pursuing her own interests, an ultimately costly compromise, Marla acquiesced ruefully, as she uneasily agreed to the doubtful pleasure of another sampling of soft-shelled crab when they met for lunch.

❦   ❦   ❦

Wandering listlessly down the narrow aisle, Reba let her fingers trail lightly across the faded spines of dusty books lining the shelves. Reading wasn't one of her favorite pastimes so she never quite understood why Naomi, and yes, even Marla, wanted to spend precious vacation time vicariously living another's adventures when there could be so much more excitement in creating one's own.

Like now, for instance, she contemplated, when she could be outside, enjoying the sunshine, mingling with the locals. Her thoughts scurried back to the Village Square where, just moments before, she and Naomi watched fishermen at their daily task of net mending. Reba, delighted to discover the handsome "Adonis" among them, was even more delighted when he glanced up from his labors and across the Square to where she and Naomi stood. A tingle of excitement shivered through her now as she remembered the bold, flirtatious grin he cast in her direction. But then, satisfied at having fulfilled her part of the earlier agreed upon itinerary for the day, Naomi quickly urged their steps away from the danger of temptation and into the musty little book store.

Reba sighed and pulled a worn book from its alphabetically assigned position on the shelf. *Maryland State Crustaceans: as taken from records of Maryland State Archives.* Leafing glumly through the tightly bound volume, she let her disinterested gaze slide over the words marching dutifully across the crisp pages. She paused, a bold typed caption demanding her attention from the top of one page. *"The Blue Crab"*: hadn't that been their lunch entrée at Mo's? Her interest now captured, Reba read further. According to this dissertation, by any other name the blue crab was know as *Callinectes Supidus*; Greek for "beautiful swimmer," Latin for "savory." Well, thought Reba, she'd have to agree with the Latinos, it did turn out to be a rather savory entrée.

She continued her perusal of the publication as it went on to advocate the use of caution with this difficult to handle crustacean, warning it could deliver an extremely painful pinch; was noted for being particularly aggressive, even out of water, lunging toward any movement considered a threat. That information brought a sardonic lift to Reba's eyebrows.

"These swimmers might be beautiful," she conceded softly, " even savory, but they obviously have a definite attitude problem."

The following lines, an excerpt lifted from a *New Science* magazine, brought a smile to Reba's lips. *"Boy crabs boogie to bring females out of hiding."* She recalled Naomi's reaction to the legend printed on Mo's menu, one she and her friends had discounted as a bit of local whimsy. *"The wild dance of the male blue crab is performed to attract would-be lovers."* Apparently, Mo's narrative had its origination from an authentic source. A quick scan of the print crawling down the page suggested the rest of the presentation was devoted to the harvesting of the blue crab, a process of no interest to Reba.

Eager to share this discovery further substantiating the antics of the blue crab, she glanced across the room to where Naomi, obviously having found a book of interest, buried her nose in its pages. With a sigh of disappointment, Reba stuffed the book featuring an expose of cavorting crustaceans back among its tired counterparts.

"This is going to be a boring afternoon," she sighed.

Reba glanced impatiently about the tiny room. It was so stuffy in this musty archive she could scarcely breathe. Coveting a breath of fresh air, she contemplated her option of stepping outside for a moment. Naomi, possibly ensconced here for the next few hours, probably wouldn't even notice her absence.

Closing the door quietly behind her, Reba greedily inhaled the aroma of pungent ocean air, grateful for its freshness after the stagnant oppressiveness inside the bookstore. Across the Square, she could see the fishermen still busy with their nets. Her eyes, eagerly probing their numbers, settled upon the brawny figure of one fisherman, the one she and her friends had dubbed "Adonis." She watched his easy movements, fascinated by tanned, sinewy fingers deftly threading new line through the torn nets, his muscled back flexing beneath the tautness of his sweat-stained tee shirt each time he tugged at the heavy webbing.

She felt her face flush when, in the next instant, her startled gaze met the blatant insolence of his. She realized, not only had she been ogling him, he'd been aware of her undisguised admiration. Struggling to control her breathing, she forced a smile in return to the salacious one he offered. Her heart stumbled as, with a curt, chauvinistic jerk of his head, he motioned her to join him.

Reba hesitated for a moment, casting a quick glance over her shoulder toward the bookstore, considering the almost certain disapproval of her friend inside. But then, what was the harm, she rationalized? After all, it was broad daylight; she was a grown woman. Slowly, if perhaps a little uncertainly, she made her way across the cobblestones until she stood smiling up into the handsome face of "Adonis."

"Well, Good Mahnin' pretty lady." The seaman's eyes traveled suggestively down the young woman's body, leaving no doubt as to his interest.

"Hi." Reba giggled self-consciously.

"Wheah's your warden?"

"She's not my warden," Reba countered with a defensive lift of her chin. "My friend is in the bookstore. She likes books." Somehow, she felt the need to explain. "We just don't always enjoy the same things."

An arrogant smirk tugged at the corner of the handsome fisherman's mouth. "I'm guessin' mebbe you and me, we might be enjoying the same things." A lascivious undertone shadowed his voice. "Any chance of you gettin' off by yourself . . . like mebbe tonight, after I get in from fishin'?"

Reba's heart fluttered. This gorgeous hunk of man was actually asking her for a date. She hesitated, disturbing thoughts of Naomi's unavoidable reaction crowding aside the ecstasy of the moment. Not only Naomi, Reba suspected even Marla would disapprove of such a liaison. *But, oh gawd, he's so gorgeous.*

"I . . . I'll think about it," Reba faltered.

"I'll see you down at the wharf, say about seven," the fisherman asserted. "Theah's a place called the Blue Crab." With a grunt of exertion, he hefted the rolled netting onto his shoulder and turned toward the docks.

Pausing, he glanced back to where Reba stood watching his departure. A smile slashed a crescent of white across his tanned face, then, adjusting the heavy webbing on his shoulder, he resumed his journey, but not before he dropped one eyelid in that familiar, slow, deliberate wink.

Lightheaded with excitement, Reba made her back way across the square. Filling her with a delicious anticipation was the recounting of her Cape Code adventure to her fellow workers back at Airline Reservations; their envious reaction when she described the handsome fisherman who'd actually asked her for a date. A small frown puckered her brow. She doubted she'd share today's adventure with Naomi, or Marla, for that matter. After all, it wasn't as if she actually planned to keep the date. Or did she? She could, of course, but should she - would she? The tiny voice of an uneasy conscience cautioned, "Perhaps not."

🍁　　　🍁　　　🍁

The musty odor of the museum's one room interior was as overpowering as Marla remembered. Pale overhead lighting failed to successfully penetrate the dimness, yet she had no difficulty in finding her destination. A few short steps across the small room brought her once again to the glass enclosure and its display of grainy photographs. She scrutinized the fuzzy image of the seaman most recently captured on low-quality film. Hands jammed in his pockets, fisherman's cap pulled low on his forehead, Jacob Mallory, captain of the Sea Nymph stared back. There was something about that serious, unsmiling face, the eyes so dark and troubled; a twinge of sadness plucked at Marla's heart. Focusing again on the caption below, she stared at the notation with its vague declaration, "presumably lost at sea." A sudden painful tightening in her chest reminded Marla, captivated in a moment of intrigue, she'd forgotten to breathe.

Greedily sucking the stagnant air into her deprived lungs, she turned her back on the disturbing display. Looking about her, she searched the recesses of the murky room for some sign of life. Surely there must be someone on duty, she thought, a curator or an attendant. A slight movement in one far corner of the room caught her eye. A bromidic old woman, appearing as ancient as the museum artifacts themselves, hunched over a poorly lighted workbench, a pair of pince-nez glasses perched precariously upon the bridge of her nose.

Moving closer, Marla saw the aged attendant was attempting to repair the yellowed pages of a tattered copy of *Maritime Piloting*. A well-worn, putrid green cardigan sweater draped about her shoulders was held in place by the tarnished faux-gold chain of a sweater guard. The old woman paused and with gnarled, arthritic fingers, impatiently tucked an errant strand of white hair into the loose chignon gathered at the nape of her neck. Then, oblivious to all but the task at hand, she returned to her labors. It is not until Marla stood directly in front of the counter and obtrusively cleared her throat, the old woman became aware of her presence.

"Good morning." Marla's greeting echoed loudly in the mausoleum-like stillness.

The aged crone glanced up, her finger-smudged eyeglasses dropping to the end of the black velvet tether secured to her bosom by a large cameo brooch. A smile creased the leathery face obviously exposed to many seasons of New England sun and wind.

"Well, sakes alive. A good mahnin' to you, too." Her voice was sharp, brittle from disuse and age, Marla suspected. "My, what a surprise, havin' a visitor here so early in the mahnin'. You're one of them folks staying out at Ed Balcom's place, his sister ain't it? You Ed's sister? My, you don't look at all like him. But maybe you took after t'other side of your family. That happens you know. Sometimes there's a whole family wheah the brothers and sisters don't look at all alike. And ain't that nice you visiting our little museum? Not like the big one in Boston, but ever bit as good. "

Whatever happened to the stoic, tight-lipped New Englanders I keep hearing about? Marla agonized. *If I don't interrupt her soon, I'm going to drown in this one-sided conversation.*

"No, no, I'm not Ed's sister," she interjected. "Just a friend, and yes, this is a lovely museum. In fact, I have some questions about one of your displays, the pictures of those earlier Cape Cod sailors."

"John Aldahwood? Captain Johnson? Both fine men, good fishermen. I knew Captain Johnson well, really well." Her eyes softened as she gazed off into a private memory known to her alone. "Fact is, he had quite a fancy for me in our youngah days." The fractured voice had grown wistful.

"And Captain Mallory?" Reluctant to intrude upon this sacred moment, Marla knew she had to move on. "Did you know him?"

The eyes that a moment ago gazed inwardly with such tenderness now hardened with suspicion. The curator's lips tightened into a thin, tight line, her knob of a chin jutted outward, accentuating tiny bristles of facial hairs that had somehow escaped the harvesting tweezers. "Why you askin' 'bout Jacob?" she demanded harshly.

"I . . . I'm just curious." Marla dipped her head toward the photo display. "It says there he was presumably lost at sea and I just wondered . . ."

"If that's what it says then that's what happened." The suddenly hostile old woman returned her attention to the tome on her workbench. "I got my own business to tend to. I 'spect maybe you might be doin' the same."

Obviously dismissed, Marla saw no choice but to retrace her steps. Careful to avoid the disturbing memorial display, she hurried across the small room and back out into the brightness of the noonday sun. Deep in thought, pondering the puzzles of the morning, she slowly made her way toward Mo's café. Her sleuthing efforts only left her more confused than before. Why, she wondered impatiently, did everyone seem so reluctant to talk about the missing fisherman? She was more determined than ever to unravel the mystery surrounding Jacob Mallory, captain of the Sea Nymph.

CHAPTER TEN

The sun dipped low on the horizon by the time they arrived back at the cottage. Before long, the golden orb would slip into the shimmering waters of Cape Cod Bay. There was still time for a walk along the beach, Marla decided. She felt a strange magnetic draw toward that abandoned cabin atop the bluff, a compulsive need to view it once more before the day ended.

"I think I'll take a stroll on the beach," she announced, "while there's still light."

"Good grief, haven't you had enough walking for one day?" Collapsing onto the couch, Naomi propped her feet upon the matching ottoman. "I'm not leaving this couch, except maybe to pour myself a glass of wine."

"I won't be long," Marla promised. "I'd like to watch the sunset from the beach."

"Ooh, that sounds nice." Reba wriggled her feet into the sandals she'd discarded but a moment before. "I'll go with you."

The last thing Marla wanted was Reba's company, or anyone else's for that matter. But she saw no way of discouraging her friend without arousing questions. She forced a smile to her lips.

"Great, let's go, then."

Marla regretted not finding some excuse for postponing her walk. Reba's chatter was constant. While Marla usually enjoyed her friend's bubbling enthusiasm, today it only interfered with her need to be alone, to sort out the thoughts plaguing her peace of mind. Half-heartedly she listened to recounts of the morning's activities.

"Guess who Naomi and I saw at the square this morning?" Reba chirped.

Like I hadn't already guessed, thought Marla.

"Remember that cute fisherman we saw the other morning? Well, he was there again today. What a hunk! I'm sure he recognized us. I think he might have spoken to me if Naomi hadn't been there. She can be such a prude some times."

Preoccupied with her own thoughts, Marla failed to notice the minutest hesitation in her companion's dissertation.

"Anyway," Reba rallied, " I'm sure he probably has a girlfriend."

Like the incessant waters of a gurgling brook, her friend's endless prattle splashed on, unheeded, across the stony abstraction of Marla's mind.

"Of course, we ended up at that old bookstore. What a musty mausoleum that is," Reba grumbled. "I did find an interesting book, though. It was all about the blue crab. Remember that stuff we read at the café the other day, about the blue crab boogie?" Not waiting for a response, she rambled on. "I guess it's really true. According to the author of the book, the male crab dances this boogie to entice the female out of hiding. Can you imagine?"

Reba paused to shake the sand out of one sandal, then hurried to catch up with her companion. "Seems to me," she continued, " it's the lady's curiosity that's her downfall. But then I suppose if some guy's doing a crazy dance in her yard, you can't blame the gal for poking her head out to see what the heck is going on. That's when Old Twinkle Toes releases this jet stream of hormonal chemical, or whatever, meant to attract the female. Works like a smoke screen, befuddles little Miss Nosey and, well, the rest is rhetoric."

Marla could hear the vacuous recitation in the background but the words no longer registered. They were nearing the spot where Marla hoped to sneak one more glimpse of the gray cabin.

Suddenly, Reba's voice, having risen an octave, penetrated the self-generated cloud buffering Marla's introspection. "Oh, look, Marla, there's a little cabin at the top of that bluff. Ugh," she grimaced. "What a dismal-looking place."

"Yes, isn't it?" The foreboding specter loomed above them.

"Oh, my gosh." The thought apparently occurred to her companion with no encouragement from Marla. "Is that where you stayed your first night here?"

"That's it."

"Wow, looks like a cousin to Bates Motel"

"That was kind of my impression, too," Marla admitted.

"Let's go up for a closer look," Reba urged.

"No can do. There's no way up from the beach," Marla blurted, then hesitated, her friend's expression warning her she might be revealing a more than a casual knowledge.

"How do you know that for sure?" Reba demanded. Then, typically Reba, she turned and, not waiting for a reply, scurried toward the foot of the bluff. "Let's go check," she called back over her shoulder. "Maybe there's a way up on the other side."

Marla saw no choice but to stumble after her. When she finally caught up with her companion, Reba had already passed the pile of logs at the foot of the bluff and was staring into a small cove just beyond.

She turned to greet Marla's approach, eyes sparkling with an I-told-you-so expression. "Look, Marla, somebody's boat. That means there must be a way up from the beach."

As the sun's red ball slithered into the gold-tinged waters, darkness quickly crowded the few lingering rays of anemic light toward the horizon. Unfettered now, wisps of fog crept stealthily across the sand. In the quickly disappearing half-light, Marla's gaze followed the direction of Reba's pointing finger to where, in a slimy pool left by the outgoing tide, the weathered remains of a fishing skiff rested upon its side. Peering through the murky twilight, she strained to make out the faded letters painted upon the peeling hull. A chill stirred the nape of her neck, crawled slowly across her scalp. Although some of the letters stenciled across its bow were no longer readable, there was no doubt this battered dinghy belonged to the missing Sea Nymph.

CHAPTER ELEVEN

With a week gone by since their arrival at the little fishing village, half the vacation was already over. It was Naomi's suggestion, since they'd exhausted inspection of the village offerings perhaps they should expand the boundaries of their browsing.

"Let's drive over to Boston today." Naomi studied the road map spread on the breakfast table before her. "I'd like to check out some of the old historical sites. What do you gals think?"

"Sounds great to me," Reba agreed, eager, as always, at the prospect of a new adventure.

Marla, on the other hand, could not rise above her obsession. "I think I'll just dork around on the beach today," she countered. "You two go on ahead."

"Oh, Marla, you should go with us," wailed Reba. "Boston will be a blast."

"Are you sure, Marla?" There was a disturbing edge of irritation to Naomi's voice. "We may end up spending the night."

"I guess I'm just a little worn out, I don't really feel up to sightseeing," Marla lied. "Really, I'll be all right. You two have fun. Call me if you decide to stay over."

It was obvious Naomi was displeased with her improvised excuse, but Marla couldn't help that. She needed time to herself, time to sort out the maze of inconsistencies surrounding the mystery that was disrupting her peace of mind. She hoped she succeeded in convincing Reba, after careful inspection of the fishing dinghy, it had simply been left on the beach as a totally "unseaworthy" derelict. However, there was something about that abandoned little boat bothering Marla, something she wasn't quite able to put her finger on. She needed to visit the cabin again, this time alone.

It was mid-morning before Naomi and Reba finally drove out the driveway, headed for the bustle of Boston. Marla stood in the doorway, waving, impatient for their departure, eager to put her own plan into action. The minute they were out of sight, she slipped into her walking shoes, a pair of sweats, and set off for her destination. It was well past noon when she arrived. She'd forgotten how much longer the distance by road. Exhausted when finally, pausing at the foot of the path, she stared up at the gray apparition holding her in its power. This time, she reminded herself uneasily, there would be no four-wheeled chariot awaiting her should she need to make a quick departure. Ignoring the warning voice of indecision, Marla set foot upon the path leading to her nemesis, determined to rid herself of its obsession.

The weathered entrance offered no resistance; as before, it was not locked. Marla hesitated, fighting a sudden wave of indecision, then, taking a deep breath to fortify her courage, stepped inside. There was no indication anyone had been inside the cabin since her last visit. She let her gaze drift idly around the room. Nothing had changed: The wood box, still filled with dry driftwood; the tiny cook stove, now cold in its disuse; the kitchen table and chairs awaiting any who would dine there. Peeking into the bedroom with its tidily made-up bed, its low dark wood ceiling accentuating the claustrophobic dimensions, Marla noticed something she'd not noticed before, a thin dirt-stained cord dangling above the doorway. Nostalgic memories crowded around her as she recognized the hidden access to an attic: a pull-down stairway. There had been one in the old house where her grandmother lived.

A tug on the cord's knotted end released the carefully concealed stairway. A disturbingly familiar sound accompanied its unfolding, an intrusive grating that triggered a twinge of uneasiness within Marla's subconscious.

She hesitated, mentally groping to identify the apprehension aroused by the unmistakable sounded of metal, grinding against metal. Then, resolutely shrugging off a strange sense of foreboding, she placed her foot on the bottom step and ascended the narrow ladder rising above her. It took a moment for her eyes to adjust to the dimness. A narrow wooden plank, placed across the crisscrossing studs and joists, led to the end of the gabled enclosure. The pale light forcing its way through a dirt encrusted window created ghostly tapestries of dusty cobwebs wafting among the rafters.

For a one delicious instant, Marla was a child again, peering cautiously into the darkness of her grandmother's mysterious attic; curious, yet terrified, by the macabre specters she imagined lurking there. Now she squinted into the musty dimness of another intimidating loft. No different than the eerie space beneath Granny's roof, she decided, just an attic. Retreating down the narrow steps, Marla returned the ladder to its place of hiding, once again disturbed by the vague familiarity of the rasping sound of metal against metal.

A midday sun flowed through the open drapes, anointing the main room with an absolving grace of light, bathing it in a warm, deceptive innocence. At that moment, Marla's fears seemed grossly unfounded, perhaps even a little senseless. When did she, usually practical, reasonably rational, allow her thinking to become so impaired, her imagination to go crazy? A sigh slipped past her lips and Marla suddenly became aware how much the long walk had tired her. Perhaps she should rest a bit before starting the long journey back. Gratefully lowering herself onto the sagging couch, Marla tucked her legs beneath her, and curling into a fetal position, let weariness close her eyes.

❦   ❦   ❦

Startled onto the verge of wakefulness, Marla perched on the edge of the couch, peering fearfully into the unfamiliar dimness of the room. Had she slept into nightfall? No, the hopsack draperies had been drawn, sometime while she slept, closing out the brightness of the sun, filling the once friendly room with shapeless, abstract shadows. Yet, it wasn't this disturbing realization or the sudden darkness frightening her. She raised her hand to where her heart fluttered in her throat. Had she dreamed it, the sensation of someone's lips pressed gently against her own?

Frantic, she crawled across the back of the couch, clutching at the coarse-woven draperies, dragging them aside. No longer held at bay, light from the afternoon sun invaded the room, probing into its corners, routing out the darkness. It was a moment before her eyes adjusted to the sudden illumination. Anxiously, Marla scanned her once again threatening surroundings. Nothing appeared to have been disturbed. Yet, the dormant cook stove, the inanimate table and chairs, once waiting in docile quiescence now seemed to hover in militant readiness. The ambiance of innocence she'd experienced earlier transformed itself into the hostile face of treacherous collusion.

Marla's immediate concern became the need to vacate this chamber of horrors. A few hasty strides brought her to the door; placed her hand upon its smooth black knob. The metal grip slipped in her moisture-laden palm. She grasped it more firmly, her frustration quickly turning to panic. The handle refused to turn. Was the door locked?

Oh lordy, lordy. She could taste the fear rising in the back of her throat. *What shall I do? What shall I do? My cell phone. Yes, yes. Bless Naomi and Reba for insisting I carry my cell phone.* Marla fumbled in the pocket of her jacket until her groping fingers closed about that comforting instrument of salvation. Impatiently, she wrested it from its snug haven. Terror disabled her stability. The phone slipped from her trembling hand, crashing against the wood floor.

"Oh, dear God," Marla whispered, "don't let it be broken."

She scooped the tiny black box from the floor, clutching it tightly in her hand, her cold fingers poised above the numbered buttons. She hesitated. *Who can I call? Not Naomi or Reba, they are miles away in Boston. Who do I know in this forsaken little outpost? Who can I call for help?*

CHAPTER TWELVE

Nine-one-one! The numbers slashed themselves across Marla's panic-numbed brain. Of course, 911. Surely those emergency digits applied, even here in this remoteness. There must be someone out there to come to her rescue. Regret for the morning's irrevocable decision taunted her. If she'd gone with Naomi and Reba, she'd be on the way to Boston now, looking forward to sharing precious time with her friends. How did she let herself get so entangled in this crazy obsession with a deserted cabin, a missing sailor?

Oh, Naomi, Reba, I promise, if I ever get out of this mess, I'll never let my curiosity ruin another vacation for us. Marla raised her fingers above tiny numbers that suddenly blurred as her eyes filled with tears of emotion. Angrily, she brushed them away and jabbed at the miniscule digits.

The telltale click as connection was made brought a flush of relief, knowing the cell phone still operated in spite of her earlier clumsiness. At least, Marla hoped that was the situation. She could hear ringing at the other end of the line. And ringing. And ringing. Why didn't someone answer? Didn't they realize this was an emergency? Giving vent to her agitation, she once again accosted the door handle with her free hand, wrenching at it as if to dissuade it from its stubborn stand.

A voice chirped into her ear. "Nine one, one."

At the same moment, the worn black knob turned in her hand. The weathered door swung open and Marla was once again standing in the warm afternoon sun, filling her lungs with the salty, iodine-tainted ocean air.

"Hello? Hello? This is Nine-One-One. Who's calling, please?"

demanded the voice from the little box still pressed against Marla's ear. "Is theah a problem?"

"Oh, yes, I mean, no. It's just that . . .." *Oh, dear. What to do now?* She couldn't say she was trespassing in Jacob's cabin, thought she'd been locked in. That was obviously not going to go well in this privacy obsessed community. "No, no, I'm sorry. Everything is okay, now. I'm sorry for troubling you. Thank you. Everything's fine, now. Thank you."

Lowering the cell phone from her ear, she quickly closed the cover. *Well, that could have been a nasty situation.* Until this moment, it hadn't occurred to Marla she could be in trouble for trespassing. As for the locked door, the knob was just stuck, she reasoned. After all, it was old, rusty, a victim of salt air and the elements. Still, she would have sworn . . ..

Marla decided it was high time she ended the day's escapade. She faced a long walk ahead of her and needed to get started if she wanted to get back to the cottage before dark. She hesitated, a tenacious curiosity, refusing to release her, suddenly reminded her of the reason she'd returned to the mesa today. The little dinghy she and Reba had discovered the day before; she wondered if it could be seen from the top of the bluff. Curiosity temporarily postponing the impending journey back to the village, Marla worked her way across the grass-covered mesa to the point from where she believed the little boat might be visible. Not sure of the earth's stability at the lip of the bluff, she dropped to her knees and cautiously crawled to where she could look down to the beach.

Reaching for the comforting security of a clump of beach grass, her hand closed about a circle of metal buried among its roots. One by one, her probing fingers disclosed a series of metal circles connected to one another. Flopping onto her stomach, she followed the chain to where it disappeared over the embankment. Peering beyond its edge, Marla discovered the chain supported a sturdy rope ladder like those seen hanging over the side of a ship. The ladder extended to the sandy beach below and the little cove sheltering the remains of the battered dinghy.

A tinkling sound erupting from the pocket of her parka demanded Marla's attention. Digging her elbows into the soft earth, she scrunched backward until she was a safe distance from the edge of the bluff. Rolling onto her side, she tugged at the cell phone in her pocket. Could 911 be calling back? A sudden unnerving thought slowed her hand as she lifted the phone to her ear. Could a call made from a cell phone actually be traced?

"Hello?" Her voice, struggling against the dryness of her throat sounded unfamiliar even to her own ears.

"Hello? Marla?"

A grateful sigh released the breath held captive in her lungs as she recognized the familiar voice. "Naomi!" Marla realized she was all but shouting in her relief. "Naomi," she added more softly. "Where are you? Are you back already?"

"No, no, we're still in Boston. Are you okay? You don't sound like you."

"Oh, I'm fine, fine. I was just surprised to hear from you."

"I gather you aren't at Ed's bungalow. Is everything okay?"

"Yes, yes, of course it is." Marla insisted. "I'm just out walking the beach."

"Well, okay." Skepticism shadowed Naomi's voice. "I'm just calling to let you know we've decided to stay the night in Boston. I wish you had come with us, Marla. There's just so much to see here. We're thinking of maybe staying a couple of nights." Naomi's tone took on a hopeful note. "Look, why don't we come back tomorrow and pick you up? I don't like you being there by yourself."

"Okay, Mother Superior, you can just stop worrying. Honest, Naomi, I'm fine. I'm really enjoying this quiet time. I think I need it more than a tourist's tour of Boston."

"Well, if you're sure."

Rolling into a yoga sitting position, Marla started to tuck her feet beneath her when a strangled gasp of surprise wrenched itself from lips suddenly gone dry. Planted squarely in front of her, commanding her direct line of vision, was one pair of very large, mud-covered boots.

"Marla? Marla? Are you still there?"

Marla forced the words past the lump of fear crowding into her constricted throat. "Yes, yes, I - I'm here. I'm fine, Naomi," she managed. "You and Reba have a good time. I'll be fine, honest."

Carefully lowering the cell phone from her ear, Marla firmly punched the disconnect button and snapped the cover closed before daring to lift her gaze from those muddy boots to the face of their owner.

Towering above her, hands braced on his hips, a scowl darkening his rugged features, was the old fisherman, the Spencer Tracy look-alike who'd been Marla's rescuer but a few days earlier. While recognition brought Marla a rush of relief, it was obvious the glowering mariner was quite displeased with her.

"You know you're trespassin'," he growled.

If she'd learned but one thing during their brief association it was honesty was the only acceptable policy with this "old man of the sea". "I know," she confessed. "And I'm sorry. I'm honestly sorry." She accepted the hand he extended and let him pull her to her feet, feeling more comfortable now that she was facing him at eye level. "There were just some things I had to know."

"You're an inquisitive one." His scowl softened. "You just might be finding more trouble than you're wantin'."

Something in his tone warned her she should say no more. It was time for her to back off. Unfortunately, minding her own business was never one of her stronger points. Once aroused, her stubborn curiosity demanded satisfaction. So, with the refinement of a bulldog gnawing at a bone, she blundered on.

"I certainly wouldn't let myself into the cabin if I thought someone lived here," she retorted. "But it was my understanding the cabin is vacant, abandoned."

The old man pursed his lips and it was a moment before he spoke. "You're right about that," he assured her. "Theah's nobody lives theah."

Common sense deterred Marla's next question, but not for long. "Then how do you explain the fact someone closed the drapes this afternoon while I slept on the couch?" Marla persisted. "And I would have sworn the door was locked when I tried to leave a few minutes ago. How do you explain that?" She decided not to share the illusion of a fleeting kiss that awakened her.

The dark scowl returned. "I 'spect the closed curtains was your own doin'," he snapped, making no effort to hide an inference of her probable memory lapse. "As for the door handle . . . " His jaw clamped shut, biting off unspoken words.

Marla was tempted to ask about his timely, unexplainable appearance at the cabin but realized she'd already gone too far, overstepped an invisible boundary. She was, after all, the trespasser.

" Look, I'm truly sorry if . . ." Involuntarily, she reached out in a gesture of apology, touched Jeremiah's shoulder, then quickly withdrew as she felt his muscles tighten beneath her hand.

When he spoke again, the gruffness of the old man's voice reflected the anger in his eyes. "I'm tellin' you once more, Miss, go back to your own kind before you make trouble for yourself. Snoopin' outsiders ain't welcome heah."

Earlier, upon discovery of the fisherman's ladder, Marla rashly considered the doubtful merits of thus lowering herself to the beach in order to take the shorter route home. While she dreaded the long walk back to the cottage by way of the seemingly endless road, the sobering contemplation of dangling above the possibility of an incoming tide quickly relegated that alternate plan to the "maybe not" file. Now, of course, she knew she had no choice other than the route originally bringing her there.

Consideration of her options dissipated as, with no attempt at false courtesy, her disgruntled companion firmly escorted her to the path leading her away from the mesa and any hopeful resolution of her unanswered questions.

Dutifully, Marla directed her feet along the dusty trail, keeping her eyes focused ahead until she reach the graveled roadway. Glancing back over her shoulder, she could see the old man still standing at the bluff's edge, monitoring her banishment. Startled, she stumbled, her knees seemingly no longer able to support her. There, standing but a few feet behind her evictor, another taller, slender figure witnessed her departure, his hands shoved into the pockets of his foul weather jacket, a seaman's cap pulled low over his eyes.

Marla lurched forward, struggling to regain her balance. When she looked back, both figures had disappeared.

CHAPTER THIRTEEN

The colorful explosion of daybreak had long since faded when the tinkling command of Marla's cell phone, now resting on the bedside table, awakened her. She allowed herself the luxury of a long cat-like stretch before activating the call. It was Naomi.

"Hi, just checking in. How's everything going?"

"Just fine," Marla yawned. "How are things in Boston?"

"Great! Are you sure you don't want to join us, Marla? You like early American history. You'd really enjoy Boston."

"No thanks, Naomi. I'm honestly doing fine here." Marla knew there was no way she could break away from her obsession, not now, not after yesterday's episode. "I'm getting a good rest. In fact, today is the first day I've slept in since I can't remember when."

"Well, if you're sure." There was a hesitant pause at the other end of the line. "It's just . . . you hung up so quickly yesterday. I was worried that, well . . . if you're ill, or something, we can come back today."

Oh, no, I don't want them here today. Panic snatched away the last remnants of sleep. *There are things I need to do; things I don't want to have to explain to my rationalistic friend.*

"Honest, Naomi," Marla insisted. "I'm fine. Everything's fine. You and Reba have a good time. You can fill me in on Boston when you get back. I'll be looking forward to it."

Marla wasn't sure Naomi was entirely convinced but at least she seemed to accept the proffered assurances and hung up, leaving Marla with guilt over her blatant deception of a dear friend. But she had plans for the day, plans not easily explained to a pragmatic. A reluctance to encounter the old fisherman again predicated postponement of any immediate revisit to the cabin. But his warnings had only tweaked Marla's curiosity to the point-of-no-return. More than ever, she knew she needed to find answers to the mystery surrounding that little cabin and its missing owner.

Today, she'd decided, might be a good time to seek out new, unsuspecting victims for her personal inquisition. Mentally, she perused the streets of the village, groping for the most promising respondent for her unsanctioned investigation. Who in this close-knit village, she wondered, was not intimidated by its code of secrecy? Recalling her recently unsuccessful encounter, she eliminated the obviously biased museum curator. Who, then? A tanned face winked at her from among the images recently stored in her memory bank, and she smiled. She knew exactly who it would be.

❦ ❦ ❦

Marla's first reaction was one of dismay as she approached the Village Square. The fishermen she'd expected to find there had apparently already finished the early morning chore of mending their nets. The Square was nearly empty. She berated herself for her earlier self-indulgence and the leisurely breakfast seemingly sabotaging her plans for the day. She noticed them, then, at the far side of the Square; two seamen securing a bundle of rolled webbing lying between them. Her attention fastened itself upon the younger of the two, a dark haired, jean-clad young man: the same sweat-stained tee shirt clinging to his muscled torso.

As she hurried across the salt encrusted bricks, fearful the two seamen might leave before she could detain them, Marla realized she'd given no thought how to approach this ostentatious young man. She need not have been concerned. Once he was aware of her presence, he became the aggressor.

Glancing up as Marla approached, their "Adonis", immediately adopting an arrogant hand-on-hip stance, greeted her with a lopsided grin. "Well, Good mahnin', good mahnin'"

Marla cringed inwardly as his dark eyes brazenly assessed her figure, wishing she'd donned more than shorts and a tee shirt that morning. A hasty, self-conscious peek toward the young trawler's companion confirmed that mariner's total disinterest in her presence. Marla turned her attention back to the object of her visit.

She forced a smile to her lips. "Good morning," she replied with as much contrived sweetness as she could muster. "I – I hope you don't mind my intrusion," she began awkwardly. "It's just, well I've been curious about this procedure you do, this mending of your nets. It's so very interesting to watch." Ignoring the suggestive curve of his lips, she struggled on. "Is . . . is it something you have to do every day?"

Marla's unsuspecting corroborator settled against the low brick wall, propping his hip upon the edifice in that familiar slouch of male nonchalance. "Oh, yes indeedy, Ma'am. Just as important as shavin', showerin',and," a mischievous twinkle danced in his eyes, "makin' love to a woman."

Marla felt her face redden at his brazen insinuation and began to wonder if she was going to be able to carry out her plan. It was taking a turn she hadn't anticipated. But she'd come too far to back out now.

"My, I had no idea." She widened her eyes in innocent admiration. "Is mending these nets a morning chore, then, before the boats can go out?"

"Every mahnin', for us trawlers, that is."

"Oh, really?" effused Marla, relieved to have altered the direction of the conversation. "Trawlers you say? Is that different from other fishing boats?"

"Theah's the trollers." The young fisherman waded arrogantly into his role as educator. "They ain't rigged for net fishin'. They do theah fishin' with lures, sometimes plugs."

"Plugs?" Marla continued to feed his hungry ego, wondering how to move the subject on to the purpose of her visit, one Jacob Mallory.

"Plugs is fish-shaped lures made outta wood. Gotta three-pronged hook out the back."

"Oh, yes. I think I saw some of those over at the museum." Grasping her moment of opportunity, Marla hurried on. "What a fascinating place that is. So many interesting displays, and oh, those poor men, lost at sea."

"Ayup. It happens." "Adonis" was obviously losing interest now that the attention turned from him.

It's now or never, Marla decided. "Did you know any of them?"

she urged. "There was one there, more recent than the others, a Jacob Mallory of the Sea Nymph. Did you know him?"

"Mebee." The indifferent shrug of his shoulders told her their conversation was nearing its end. Her informant slipped from his perch, his gaze searching the space over Marla's shoulder. "Wheah's your friend today?"

She had no doubt he was referring to Reba. "Oh, they went to Boston for a couple of days. They'll be back, maybe tomorrow."

"Hmm. Well, I gotta get back to work. Fish ain't waitin' for nobody."

Marla realized she was losing her intended respondent. "You know," she offered quickly, "I talked to a fellow yesterday who does remember this Jacob Mallory; an elderly fisherman living down on the beach."

A now disinterested "Adonis," stooping to lift one end of the bundle of netting, glanced back over his shoulder. "Oh, that'd be Jeremiah, Jacob's old man."

Speechless for a moment, Marla watched the retreating figure of her unwitting collaborator. Then, impulsively, "I'll tell Reba you asked about her," she shouted after him.

White teeth flashed in the handsome bronzed face turned toward her as one eye-lid dropped in a slow deliberate wink.

CHAPTER FOURTEEN

An excited chill of success shivered through Marla as she made her way back to the cottage. Jacob's father! Of course, it all made sense now: the defensiveness, the protective watchfulness over the cabin, the reluctance to discuss a son lost at sea. It seemed her snooping was paying off; she finally possessed the answers she'd been seeking. Almost giddy with relief, she chose to ignore the malevolent whispers of the skeptic lurking within her subconscious. The man on the path to the cabin, watching as she drove away . . . probably just old Jeremiah. But yesterday there were two men, she remembered. She shushed the inner Doubting Thomas threatening to rob her of her deliverance. She intended to enjoy her vacation, or what was left of it.

Her grousing stomach advised her lunchtime was nearing as she headed up the driveway leading to the cottage. Hungrily anticipating a foray of the refrigerator, she dug into her pocket for the house key. About to insert the notched bit of metal into the lock, she realized the door stood partially open. She was certain she'd closed it before she left that morning; thought she'd even locked it. Maybe the latch didn't catch, though somehow her mind was unwilling to accept that possibility. Still, it seemed the only probability . . . unless someone . . ..

Oh lordy. What if someone has broken into the cabin, or worse yet, walked in because I left the door unlocked? How will I explain it to Naomi's brother? Cautiously, Marla stepped across the threshold and peered into the tiny, spotless kitchen. Everything appeared to be in order.

But wait, maybe it's Ed. Marla's mind scrambled frantically for some resolution. *Maybe Naomi's brother decided to pay an unexpected visit.* She quickly extended her inspection into the living room. Temporarily mollified to find nothing disturbed, she pushed open the door to her bedroom.

The consolatory sigh about to leave her lips mutated into a strangled gasp. Someone had been in her room! Closet doors gaped open; invaded bureau drawers revealed their violated contents. Panic directed Marla's footsteps as she hastened across the hall to the room shared by Naomi and Reba. Their sleeping quarters still retained its pristine neatness. Only Marla's privacy had been usurped. What on earth of hers, she wondered, could possibly be of interest to anyone?

She made a quick inspection of her belongings. Nothing seemed to be missing, her costume jewelry, certainly of little value to anyone but herself, still rested in her travel case. What, then, was the intruder searching for? In any case, she knew she should notify the police. She turned toward the bedside table. Only then did she discover her cell phone gone.

❦   ❦   ❦

Curled in the protective arms of Ed's overstuffed chair, Marla watched as a brilliant orange sun slipped from sight. Now, only the fading light of day, lingering on the horizon, illuminated the small living room. Marla made no move to turn on the lamp beside her. An earlier attempt disclosed an unexplainable absence of electricity in this isolated, beachfront abode. The chilled glass of Vouvray in her hand did little to allay her anxiety, as had her frantic visit to the local police station.

"Probably just some beach combah," was their dismissal of her reported burglary, a seemingly standard local explanation, Marla chafed, for the unexplainable.

Reference to the sudden lack of power evoked the same lack of interest. "Happens all the time around heah;" the lethargic response. "Just be patient. It'll come back on by itself, soonah or latah."

There was little Marla could do now but sit in the semi-darkness and "just be patient" wondering if whoever had her cell phone would respond when Naomi called, which she was certain to do. Marla could only imagine the resulting alarm for her ever-tolerant companions. She berated herself for, once again, having failed to keep that instrument of communication on her person and cringed at the mental anguish her carelessness would cause.

Silhouetted dunes of sand became merely dark, undistinguishable mounds while spiky tufts of beach grass totally disappeared in the dimness of approaching evening. Reluctant to surrender to its restrictions, Marla peered into the darkness, straining for one last glimpse of the familiarity of the retreating surroundings. Tears of effort filled her eyes, blurring her vision. The bushy Scotch pine at the corner of the patio appeared to have split in two. She blinked, hoping to clear the unwelcome double vision, but the illusion did not dissolve. Annoyed, she blinked again, then realized her eyes were not playing tricks upon her.

The figure of a man silhouetted itself against the glass panels of the doorway. Even in the pale light, Marla could distinguish the fisherman's cap pulled down upon his forehead, hands, tucked deep into the pockets of his jacket, before he disappeared into the shadows.

The wineglass fell from her inert fingers spilling its pale yellow contents onto the earth tones of the berber carpet. Shock severed all communications between her brain and motor functions. Frozen into immobility, she stared into the black void beyond the darkened patio. Silent screams of terror ricocheted inside her head.

Maybe he didn't see me, sitting here in the dark. Her threatened logic clutched at the fragile straw of the improbable. *But, what if he did? Did I lock the back door?* Marla knew she should check, but dared not move.

She sensed his presence, then, knew he was in the room. She heard his shallow breathing, was aware he now stood behind her chair. Her entire being shriveled into one frightened lump cowering at the back of her throat.

"Please, don't be afraid." His voice, husky, re-assuring, came as a whisper. "I mean you no harm."

Marla's frantic brain urged her to leap to her feet and run, to escape this intruder. Fear pinioned her immobilized body to the cushions of the lounger. Ruthlessly, she dug her fingers into the soft fabric of the chair arms, struggling against the reflexes of hysteria.

"Theah's so much you wouldn't understand, Miss," the soft voice continued, "so much that could cause you trouble."

There was a pause. Marla heard only his breathing. Her body stiffened as, suddenly, she felt a lock of her hair being lifted from her shoulder, felt it slip gently through the intruder's fingers. She held her breath, not daring to move.

"I don't want that for you, Miss." A note of pleading entered the man's voice. "It'd be best if you just go on home."

In the silence that followed, Marla heard only her own breath hacking its ragged journey through the dryness of her throat. He was gone. Still, she dared not move.

She wasn't sure how many minutes she sat, imprisoned by her fear, maybe ten, perhaps fifteen. She might have remained there the entire night had it not been for the sudden illumination filling the room. As predicted, the electricity came back on by itself. Rising on shaky legs, Marla stumbled into the kitchen, headed for the unlocked back door. It was then she noticed it, lying upon the kitchen counter: her cell phone.

CHAPTER FIFTEEN

Warily, Marla lifted the cell phone from its place upon the tiled counter, obviously left there for easy discovery. Anxious to make contact with her friends in Boston, she flipped open the cover to check her incoming messages. Knowing Naomi, it was inconceivable to imagine any less than a dozen indignant directives awaiting, chiding Marla for not having returned her calls. Yet guilt and self-reproach took second place to eagerness as Marla's trembling fingers hovered above the digits. Oddly there was no response from the palm-sized communicator; its little screen remained dark.

Emerging from the corner of her subconscious, an uneasy thought tiptoed across Marla's mind, the possibility someone may have chosen to delete her messages. It took only a few frantic moments to discover the true problem. The battery had been removed from its compartment.

Refusing to allow herself to be intimidated by the ominous implications, she snapped the cover shut and slipped the cell phone into the security of her jeans pocket. Tomorrow she would just have to shop for battery replacements. Meanwhile . . .

It was well past the hour Marla usually retired. Since television was not one of the intrusive commodities Ed had chosen to include in his beachfront hideaway, there was little to do after dark. A late night walk was out of the question. She hesitated to turn off the electricity so recently restored. She wasn't ready to accept the darkness it had dispelled, having uneasily concluded by now, the loss of power had not been a malfunction of the power company but one involving only the cottage. Closing the drapes, Marla checked to make sure all the windows and doors were locked. Wrapped in the comforter from the foot of the bed, she sought sanctuary within the protective arms of the overstuffed easy chair. Glancing toward the lamp table beside her, Marla noticed the book Naomi had been reading. Attempting to concentrate on some author's contrived plot held little appeal for Marla at the moment, but then perhaps it would help pass the long sleepless hours until morning. She lifted the paperback from its resting place and scanned the title, *New England's Ghosts; Legend or Lies*. Reluctantly she opened its pages.

✦   ✦   ✦

It was early when she awakened. The inquisitive light of the new day peeked beneath the drapes covering the patio door. Her substitute accommodations for the restless night of sleep, thanks in part to Naomi's choice of literature, proved to be less than satisfying. Legs she tucked beneath her for warmth now complained as she liberated them from their cramped confinement. Neck muscles, forced to endure long hours of supporting her sagging head, added their screams of protest to those of her twisted shoulders and abused spine. Muttering dark incantations, she limped to the bathroom where she found absolution in the hot waters of a steamy shower.

Having restored her body to a facsimile of normalcy, Marla applied herself to the task of creating a pot of coffee, one strong enough to jump-start the flow of adrenaline needed to restore her motor skills. That having been accomplished, she felt ready to face the day. First on her agenda was the reactivation of her cell phone. A quick consultation with her watch suggested it might be too early to find any shops open in the village.

Last night's disturbing reading material lay open upon the table. Marla chose to ignore the option it offered. To appease her impatience, she decided to fill the time with a morning stroll along the beach. The bracing freshness of invigorating ocean air soon scattered the cobwebs of the night before. She was beginning to feel like herself again. She let her feet choose the path; not surprised to discover they took her to within sight of Jacob Mallory's cabin perched atop the rocky bluff.

She could not resist the provocative siren song of her insatiable curiosity. Quickly covering the distance to the where the fickle sea discarded its ever-growing pile of rejected castoffs, Marla worked her way around the water-soaked accumulation to where she and Reba discovered the abandoned dinghy. The battered hulk appeared undisturbed since last she'd seen it. Carefully skirting the salty puddles gathered at its stern, she moved to the bow of the skiff. She tentatively ran her fingers across the peeling paint: traced the few surviving letters left on its hull, while visually inspecting the small craft.

Although it appeared to have weathered many storms, she could find no evidence of any structural damage. The whispers of doubt harassing her had been silenced, her suspicions confirmed. Contrary to her conciliatory assurances to Reba, the dinghy was definitely still seaworthy.

Turning her attention away from this disquieting discovery, Marla peered into the tangle of tenacious foliage crawling up the crag's intimidating wall. Barely visible, just beyond the reach of her eager fingertips, the bottom rung of a ship's ladder dangled tantalizingly above her. Until now, it had not been her plan to ascend the ladder, but it occurred to her, this secondary means of reaching the mesa might also provide proof how someone could have been outside the cabin window that frightening evening nearly two weeks ago.

There had to be an explanation, unless she was dealing with one of New England's legendary ghosts. With the possibility of discovery only a few inches away, she found herself looking about for something to stand upon. This unorthodox means of access was obviously provided for someone much taller than she was.

Her search for a makeshift booster proved futile. Unless she could drag the dinghy closer to the base of the bluff, or perhaps wrestle a log away from its water-soaked companions, it seemed there was no possible way she could reach the ladder. She had no choice but to abandon her efforts, for the time being, or at least until she could arrive at a more feasible solution. Meanwhile, there was the alternative of resuming her morning beach walk.

The tide was out so it was an easy stroll to the jumbled pile of castaway flotsam. A partially buried log, bleached white by the sun, worn smooth by the wind and sand, provided a perfect perch from where she could gaze out across the bay. Though its waters were restless, there was something soothing about the constancy of its waves, their tenacity as they doggedly kneaded the beach, eternally committed to metamorphose of tiny pebbles into grains of sand. Yielding to the spell of their hypnotic regularity, Marla let her thoughts drift back over the disturbing events of the past few days.

She'd been certain she'd found the answer to all the perplexities hounding her when she learned Jeremiah, the old seaman, was Jacob's father. She'd convinced herself he must have been the cabin's intruder; had reached the bluff by the hidden ship's ladder. While she still didn't know how he'd accessed the interior of the barricaded cabin, she was sure it could be easily explained as the actions of a protective father, guarding the memory and possessions of his departed son.

But after last evening, all her "probable" conjectures crumbled like sandcastles before the incoming tide. Who had stolen her cell phone and why? And the evening's mysterious intruder, obviously the one who'd returned the cell phone, was he also been the one who removed its battery? Was there some intended message in all this, a warning? An involuntary chill shivered through Marla as she recalled that eerie presence of the night before, the sound of that soft, husky voice. "So much you wouldn't understand, so much that could cause you trouble." The rhythmic waves lost their power to mesmerize. Marla rose quickly from the log and turned back toward the village. She found herself hoping Naomi and Reba had returned from Boston; were waiting for her at the cottage. She no longer wished to be alone.

A quorum of seagulls, gathering offshore for their morning conference, noisily adjourned its meeting, each constituent gliding upward on effervescent wings toward what Marla imagined to be their daily assigned patrol. She paused to watch, captivated as always by the grace of their flight. When she returned her attention to her own destination, she discovered she was not alone on the beach.

In the distance, near the debris she'd just left, someone else paused to witness this fascinating avian ritual. The space between them was enough that Marla couldn't be sure of the gender but from the stance and carriage, she suspected her cohort to be male. She felt a kinship with, actually welcomed, the presence of the early riser who shared the misty morning with her. Experiencing the need for human contact, she raised her hand and waved. The beach walker did not respond but, instead, turned away.

Marla felt she could relate to that need for solitude. It was often why she retreated to the quiet serenity of the beach. She resumed her journey at a leisurely pace, assuming if her reticent comrade desired companionship, he would make the effort to catch up with her. She glanced hopefully over her shoulder. Like her shadow, tracing her path, he paused now as she paused, turning back toward the bay. Marla shrugged her shoulders, abandoning any thoughts she might have entertained of a possible friendly verbal interchange.

She quickened her steps, preoccupied with the anticipation of a third cup of coffee awaiting her. It was only when she glanced once again over her shoulder she realized her beach mate had also increased his pace to match hers. Uneasiness invaded the tranquility of her morning stroll. Was she being followed? Why would someone be following her? She was uncomfortably reminded of the useless cell phone nestled in her jeans pocket.

CHAPTER SIXTEEN

The sight of the cottage did not bring the reassurance Marla had expected. Encouraged by the unshakable shadow at her heels, memories of last night's intrusion crowded back into her thoughts. She found herself reluctant to re-enter what should have been her haven of security. She decided, instead, to continue on to the village where, hopefully, she'd be able to restore the function of her cell phone and find temporary asylum from her growing apprehension. Only when she reached the outskirts of the village did she look back over her shoulder. Her "shadow" had disappeared.

Frustration growing with each unsuccessful visit to nearly every shop in the village, Marla finally surrendered to the abortion of her ill-fated search for seemingly non-existent cell phone batteries. Whether it was, as she suspected, a combined effort by the locals to shut her out or just this town's pre-twenty-first century existence, she'd have to locate a public phone if she wished to contact Naomi and Reba.

After many long minutes of verbal sparring with the local operator, she was at last connected to Naomi's cell phone number and braced herself for the chastising she was about to receive. Pre-planned contrition gave way to anxiety when, after six rings, there was still no response. She disconnected, reluctantly facing another battle with an uncompromising go-between before gaining access into Reba's code. She never imagined she could be so happy at the sound of a voice.

"Oh, hi, Marla. I'm so sorry we haven't called you." For a moment, Marla was taken aback by Reba's apology. "I know you've probably been trying to reach us," her friend conceded. "To tell the truth, I've had my phone turned off. You must've been worried sick and I'm so sorry."

Marla ignored a tiny twinge of conscious as Reba prattled on, relieving her of the opportunity to let her friend off guilt's hook. "You won't believe what happened yesterday. We should've called you, but everything was so wild. I'm not supposed to tell you this but Naomi forgot to take her cell phone with her when we stopped for lunch.

"While we were in the restaurant, someone stole the car along with her phone and our luggage. They've caught the guy, some transient, but we have to stick around to reclaim our belongings." Reba paused, but only long enough to replenish her oxygen supply. "We're at the police station now," she rallied. "We're going to have to spend another day here until things get straightened out. Will you be okay?"

"Well, of course I'll be okay. But what an awful thing to have happen," Marla commiserated. "I'm glad they caught the man. I won't expect you, then, until at least tomorrow." Marla wondered if she should pass along the details of someone breaking into Ed's cottage, about her cell phone being stolen. She decided to wait. They had enough on their plate right now. "You won't be able to reach me until I find some new batteries for my cell phone. But don't worry about me," she lied. "Everything here is just fine."

"Oh, and Marla." Reba's voice intercepted a disconnection. "Don't tell Naomi I told you about her cell phone, about her forgetting it. She'd be, you know, upset."

"Don't worry, Hon." Reba's inclination to "speak now, think later" came as no surprise to Marla. "Your secret is safe with me."

Marla's reassurance seemed to satisfy Reba. The communication ended with a click followed by dead air space.

Marla returned the receiver to its cradle. It seems she was to have another day to herself, another day for private sleuthing. Right now she wasn't certain how she felt about that. Yesterday, she might have been pleased at the prospect of a few more hours without interference from her friends. But after the unsettling events of the past few days, she had to admit she would welcome the comfort of their companionship.

Reluctant to return to the cottage, unwilling to resume her fruitless search for batteries, the prospect of a long aimless day stretched before her. Tantalizing odors drifting from the restaurant across the street reminded Marla she'd not eaten breakfast.

"Well," she decided, "I guess it's a place to begin."

❦   ❦   ❦

She was really going to have to control her appetite for this irresistible Cape Cod cuisine. The fitted suits hanging back in her Seattle closet were not going to take kindly to many more meals like the one she'd just indulged: lobster rolls and New England clam chowder followed by a cranberry muffin slathered with homemade blueberry jam. At least the hearty brunch placated her irritability and she could entertain the idea of returning to the cottage in a more philosophical frame of mind.

Her thoughts drifted back to the delightful experience of her sumptuous breakfast. How was it the waitress said they prepared that jam, 'sun dried blueberries stirred in copper pots with a generous lacing of vodka?'

"No wonder I'm in such a good mood," Marla chuckled.

Her path took her past the tiny museum. She was tempted, for a moment, to enter, to visit once again that disturbing display of missing fishermen or, more specifically, the haunting photo of one "presumably lost" Jacob Mallory. Indecision had her dallying upon the doorstep. She was reluctant to destroy her present euphoria, vulnerable to the temptation of procrastination. Perhaps, if the hours of the day became restless, she could return later. *Still, as long as I'm here . . .*

Apathetic low-wattage bulbs grudgingly diffused the gloomy interior with their sickly light. The curator seated at the only well-lit spot in the room glanced up from her desk. Marla was pleased to note it wasn't the same old crone who so ungraciously dismissed her on her previous visit, but, instead, a younger, less hostile appearing attendant. The young woman returned Marla's smile with one of her own then, with a narcissistic flip of her long blonde ponytail, reverted her attention to the book-mending task before her.

Marla simulated an aimless wandering among the musty artifacts, pausing casually in front of her only interest in this collection, the memorial display. The celluloid reproduction of Jacob Mallory was as she remembered it: dark brooding eyes, a face reflecting an expression of melancholy sadness. Forcing herself to turn away from the photos, she glanced toward the young curator who now eyed her with ill-concealed curiosity.

"An interesting collection," Marla offered. She pointed toward the picture she'd just been studying. "This Jacob Mallory, did you happen to know him?"

The youthful forehead gathered itself into a frown and Marla could see indecisiveness had now become the girl's council.

"I think I met his father the other day, " Marla hurried on, "down on the beach."

Hostility began to edge its way into the young clerk's expression, now vacillating between suspicion and uncertainty. "I'm just helpin' while Miss Sarah's out," she parried. "She'll be back in a few minutes. You might wanna wait and talk to her."

"I'm staying at Ed Balcom's cottage," Marla quickly explained, "with his sister."

A smile of relief washed away the doubt smudging the young woman's face. "Oh, I heard someone was staying theah. That must've been Jeremiah you met. He looks after the place for Mr. Balcom when he's gone." A tiny frown revisited her brow as the youthful substitute contemplated whether she had divulged more than her subordinate position permitted.

Marla decided it was time for her to leave, now that she knew who else has a key to their vacation cottage.

❦   ❦   ❦

Basking innocently in the mid-morning sun, the cottage exuded an aura of welcome and Marla wondered at the foolish uneasiness discouraging her from returning earlier. She refused to dwell on doubts that recently carried her to the edge of paranoia. She was ready to stretch out on the patio lounge, and while not quite ready to return to Naomi's choice of literature and the contemplation of the authenticity of New England's legendary ghosts, she looked forward to just relaxing and soaking up some rays. She inserted the house key into its counterpart only to discover the door already unlatched. Uneasiness revisited her once again: the indignity of the last invasion still fresh in her mind. Marla tried to remember; did she forget to lock up before she left that morning? Considering the state of mind she'd been in, it was entirely possible.

The living room was dark. Positive she'd opened the drapes before she left, Marla felt apprehension nibbling peevishly at the edge of an earlier complacency. Someone had been in the cottage during her absence; of that she was certain. Thanks to the young museum attendant, she now knew who possessed an extra key. All thoughts of an afternoon of leisure evaporated beneath a sudden flash of indignation. Stomping across the room, Marla yanked upon the drapery cord. *How dare Jeremiah be so presumptuous?* Was he so devoid of common courtesy, he could blatantly ignore the privacy of their even short-term tenancy?

Marla's fingers froze upon the cord, the drapes half open. Light filtering into the room fell upon the overstuffed chair serving as her bed the night before. Snagging her attention was the object resting upon its cushion. It took but a moment to identify the incongruous bit of cloth, a cap, a fisherman's cap, insolently occupying the space where she'd restlessly spent those long, uneasy hours of the night. Anger, not fear, dictated her reaction as she snatched up the well-worn bit of headgear.

Well, that does it! She was tired of playing his game. It was time she and Jeremiah had a confrontation.

       🍁   🍁   🍁

Fueled by the heat of irritation, Marla covered the familiar distance along the beach in less time than usual. The offending cap, crushed into a ball inside her parka pocket, only nurtured her fury, lengthening her stride, until she stood at the base of the bluff. For some inexplicable reason, her intuition arbitrarily determined this was where she'd find Jeremiah; the little gray cabin would be where a confrontation took place. Now, staring helplessly up the insurmountable sheerness of the rock wall, Marla faced the futility of her impetuous journey with the tardy recollection it was not possible to reach the mesa from the beach.

Chagrin became her derisive companion as she moved to where the ship's rope ladder dangled tantalizingly out of reach. A simmering combination of frustration and annoyance dissolved into shocked disbelief. The ladder no longer swung just beyond her outstretched fingertips. A wooden box, it's label rendered nearly undistinguishable by the abusive sea, rested beneath the ladder's bottom rung. Uncertainty now hovered at Marla's elbow, but only for a moment. Stepping onto the box, she closed her hand about the abrasive twist of hemp.

It took a very short time to prove, or rather disprove her challenged prowess as a seaman. The cord bit cruelly into the tender skin of her hands as she struggled to secure her feet on each elusive rung of the swaying contraption. Each breath became a painful gasp. Each step seemed only to lengthen the distance to her destination. Desperation alone kept her clinging to the rope ladder. Anger had long since deserted her, leaving only serious doubts as to the outcome of her recklessness. She began to despair of ever reaching the top until, with one last heroic surge of adrenaline she was at eye level with the mesa, staring at a browning tuft of sea grass . . . and a pair of muddied boots planted firmly upon the bluff's edge.

Dismay momentarily welded her cramped fingers to the coarse lanyard as a tanned hand suddenly entered her line of vision. *Oh, no*! Her silent screams of protest sparred with impulsive shouts of victory, which, only a seconds ago, clamored for release. This was definitely not how she'd intended to confront Jeremiah, not being at such a demeaning, demoralizing disadvantage. In her exhausted, benumbed state, it occurred to Marla, once he'd pried her from her dubious line of safety, might not Jeremiah simply decide to put an end to her prying and merely let her drop to the beach below? Ignoring the dire warnings of paranoia, Marla clutched frantically at the callused hand, wriggled her body free from the ladder and across the soggy, but welcome, dampness of the earth.

Before she could surrender to an urge to submerge herself in the euphoric waves of relief, his other hand at her elbow, her rescuer was lifting her to her feet. Only then did she look up, prepared to offer a contrite "thank you" to, she suspected, a very angry Jeremiah. Her heart suddenly ceased to function; her breath became entrapped in her throat as she recognized those sun-tanned features hovering only inches above her.

It was not the weathered face of Jeremiah, staring back at her, dark eyes filled with concern. It was, instead, the face of one Jacob Mallory, captain of the Sea Nymph, presumably lost at sea.

❦   ❦   ❦

CHAPTER SEVENTEEN

Marla had no idea how much time slipped into eternity as, numbed by shock, held in the hypnotic gaze of his dark brooding eyes, she stared mutely at the apparition confronting her. Taller, perhaps, than he appeared in his photograph, thinner maybe, but there could be no doubt it was the same seaman commemorated on the wall of the museum. Above the paleness of his face, his dark hair, no longer captured beneath a fisherman's cap, tangled in the playful fingers of a gentle breeze.

No words passed between them, yet a strange, unexplainable communication existed. Oddly, Marla knew no fear. Only when he turned away and moved toward the cabin did Marla recover her mobility, if not, she speculated later, her good sense. Several long determined strides carried the young captain the distance to his destination. There he paused. A glance in Marla's direction told her she was to follow. Without thought or reasoning, she stumbled after his tall, lithe figure, passed obediently through the portal left open for her. Closing the weathered door behind her, she turned to face her rescuer. Sudden hysteria bubbled beneath the quickening beat of her heart.

The room was empty.

Marla's frantic gaze scanned the small space, anxiously probing its shadowy corners in search of her elusive companion, her fragile shield of courage wavering before an onslaught of uncertainty and foreboding. Was she hallucinating, had her terrible obsession finally robbed her of her sanity? He'd been here, the "presumably lost at sea" captain of the Sea Nymph. He'd been here! She'd seen him! For some insane reason, the title of the book Naomi had been reading, *Ghosts of New England*, intruded upon Marla's thoughts. A chill shuddered down her spine. She crowded the implication from her mind. Her rescuer could not be a ghost. There was substance to the hand helping her up the ladder. Panic now became her mentor. Perhaps he slipped into the bathroom, she rationalized, or maybe… Her attention skittered to the opposite side of the room. There, beyond the open bedroom door, the lowered stairway leading to the attic was clearly visible.

Adrenaline surged through her body, recharging a temporarily dormant curiosity, now tingling in anticipation. Marla felt certain she was about to finally receive answers to the nattering questions plaguing her star-crossed vacation. Hastily crossing the room, she eagerly ascended the ladder into the musty attic.

Expectantly, Marla peered into the dank interior, but was rewarded with only disappointment. The attic appeared no different than when she first discovered it, and as before, she was alone. She glanced toward the only source of light in the dimly lit space and her heart broke cadence. The window she'd observed during her earlier inspection now stood open. Splintered, aged wood clawed at her shins, cloying cobwebs tangled in her hair as, crawling on hands and knees across the narrow rough planks bridging the exposed joists, Marla floundered her way to the far end of the gabled enclosure.

Out of breath, she clutched an overhead rafter with one hand and, unable to resist the overwhelming urge, frantically raked fingers through her hair where she was certain the crawly critters once residing in the clinging cobwebs now sought refuge. Only partially satisfied, Marla inched forward and grasped the security of another rafter before poking her head out the small glass-paned opening. Hopefully, she scanned the mesa for the fisherman's lean, coated figure. There was no sign of him, or of any living creature for that matter. Where could he have gone? How could he have disappeared so quickly? Puzzled, she glanced toward the earth surrounding the cabin. It was surely a ten-foot drop to that grassy surface.

Disappointed, Marla turned back toward the attic when she noticed a row of wooden cleats, nailed to the side of the building. Carefully spaced, they provided a rough, makeshift ladder to the ground below. Constant exposure to wind and sea air rendered them barely discernable from the apathetic gray of the cabin's weathered shingles.

The thought of attempting the climb down occurred to Marla but was quickly discarded. Her traumatic experience on the rope ladder remained too fresh in her mind. Foot and hand holds on that swaying contraption were at least available, if elusive, but as far as she could determine, this improvised excuse for a ladder provided little more than inadequate toe holds with no visible security grips to aid safe descent.

Disappointment once again deflated her enthusiasm. She saw no choice but to retrace her awkward journey across the joists and retreat down the narrow steps of the folding stairway. Back in the cold unfriendliness of the cabin, Marla faced a new flock of confusing doubts which, like petulant seagulls worrying the carcass of a hapless fish, swooped to assail the increasingly fragile shell of her sanity.

Still, she had to admit some of the mysteries once baiting her insatiable curiosity were no longer mysteries. Beach access to the mesa was a possibility now with the discovery of the rope ladder dangling from the bluff. Entry through the cabin's barricaded door became a simple feat, if one wished to consider the strips of wood climbing the wall outside the attic window. No longer of pressing importance, her earlier anxieties became trivial by comparison as new, more ominous inconsistencies dominated her thoughts.

The elusive Jacob Mallory: was it he who placed the box beneath the ladder so she might reach its bottom rung and gain access to the plateau? Was it his intention she would follow him, subsequently discover the attic window and the cleats marching up the side of the cabin? The wily worm of suspicion wriggled through a muddling sludge of doubts. Was all this an effort to substantiate the flimsy, over worked and, as far as she was concerned, non-existent beachcomber theory in the hope she'd abandon her prying and go home?

But that didn't explain why Jacob chose to just disappear a few moments ago, argued an inconsolable rationale. Furthermore, why did everyone insist Jacob Mallory was dead, lost at sea, when only moments ago he stood beside her, held her hand in his? A restless imagination nibbled at the edge of her logic. Could it be possible she was dealing with a ghost? *No!* She refused to entertain such an erratic supposition. There must be a more credible explanation, and she intended to find it.

Frustration knotted Marla's stomach, throbbed at her temples.

Perhaps it was the chill inside the cabin; she shivered, became aware of iciness immobilizing her fingers. Slipping them into the warmth of her parka pocket, her right hand encountered an unexpected obstruction. Pulling forth a lump of material filling the cavity, Marla stared at the crumpled fisherman's cap responsible for her impetuous journey to the cabin. The image of a tangle of dark hair tossing in the ocean winds flashed before her. Sudden awareness drew a gasp from her lips. This wasn't Jeremiah's cap after all. It belonged, instead to Jacob Mallory. An unexpected sensation, one she was not quite ready to put a name to, fluttered in the vicinity of Marla's heart. She turned the headgear in her hands, gently ran her finger across the stained sweatband.

Reluctantly, she lowered the cap onto the kitchen table where she felt assured Jacob, ghost or whatever he might be, would be certain to find it. Her hand rested for a moment on the worn, salt-stained piece of wool. She let her mind replay lingering memories of those lean features, the dark brooding eyes, until, from somewhere far offshore, the mournful moan of a ship's foghorn jolted her back to reality. Snatching her hand from the disquieting bit of cloth, she sucked a quivering breath of air into her lungs. It was time to get out of this place.

The penetrating chill inside the cabin followed her as she stepped into the dampness waiting outside. The wind seemed stronger now, more aggressive. Marla pulled her parka closely about her. Tugging the Gortex hood over her head, she turned toward the trail leading down from the mesa.

A sudden, overwhelming weariness dropped like a too-heavy mantle across her shoulders as she contemplated the long trek back to the cottage. The shorter, more appealing route would be along the beach. Except for one thing. She'd have to tackle the rope ladder again. Marla glanced down the rutty trail and the graveled road stretching beyond. She'd already managed the challenge of ascending the ladder, she reasoned. Surely, its descent should be much easier. Yet, even before she reached the lip of the embankment, she could hear the rhythmic slap of the waves as salty waters flung themselves against the sheer rock wall. While she's been chasing the elusive Captain Mallory, the tide had come in.

"Well," she muttered testily, " I guess that eliminates that option."

While it removed the trauma of traversing that swinging monstrosity, it still left Marla facing the unpleasant prospect of the blister-producing journey back along the roadway. It occurred to her, perhaps if she waited until the tide went out . . . it couldn't be more than three or four hours from now before the tide changed, or at least until the waters receded enough to expose a navigable strip of beach. She deemed that idea as much more appealing. Besides, she rationalized, by then she'd be more rested, maybe even willing to consider the alternate long way home.

Letting herself back into the cabin's dank interior, Marla purposely averted her eyes from the wool cap resting atop the table, the disturbing emotions it invoked, and moved directly to the bedroom. Snatching the wool blanket folded across the foot of the bed, she quickly stepped back into the main room and closed the door. She had no desire to be reminded of the attic access that claustrophobic chamber harbored. Wrapping herself in a shroud of gray wool, Marla flopped onto the couch, tucked her feet beneath her and settled in to wait for the tide to change.

❦   ❦   ❦

Unwilling to leave the euphoria of sleep, she snuggled into the warmth of her wool cocoon, lazily studying seemingly unfamiliar surroundings. It took a moment before awareness returned and she identified the cabin's interior. In spite of a belated recognition, her disoriented senses warned her of something different in her temporary lodgings. She pushed the blanket aside and sat up. The room was warm. A fire crackled in the once-cold cook stove. Instantly alert, Marla quickly scanned the small room. The bedroom door was still closed, just as she'd left it. Her eyes darted quickly to the kitchen table and an involuntary shudder crossed her shoulders. The table was bare, the fisherman's cap, gone.

Unexplainably, Marla felt a sharp pang of regret, a disappointment at having missed the sea captain who was obviously there while she slept. How long had she been asleep? A disquieting dimness about the room belied the four o'clock hour indicated by her watch. She glanced toward the window where a dull gray, impenetrable fog pressed against the pane.

Fully awake now, she struggled to restore her grasp upon reality when sudden recollection elbowed its way into her thoughts. Naomi and

Reba, wasn't this the day they were returning from Boston? *Oh lordy, if I'm not at the cottage . . . and they can't reach me on my defunct cell phone . . .. How will I ever explain?* Panic scattered her concentration of the moment before. *I have to get out of here, back to the cottage.* Untangling herself from the gray blanket, she stumbled across the room, yanked open the thankfully unresisting door and stepped into the smothering mist of fog enfolding the cabin.

Goaded by urgency, her reasoning distorted by desperation, it seemed to Marla her only choice would be to take the shortest route back to the cottage, even if it meant facing the challenge of that hazardous rope ladder again. Abandoning caution, she stumbled through the fathomless mist toward what she hoped was the direction of the bluff. When it seemed she'd traveled the necessary distance, she dropped to her knees, inching forward until her groping fingers came in contact, first with the metal rings staked into the ground, and then the course hemp of the ladder's top rung.

Her heart pounding in her ears, crowding into her throat, Marla knew if she did not act quickly, she would surely lose her courage. Still clutching the last of the metal rings, she turned her back and edged toward the lip of the bluff, probing the emptiness with her foot. It seemed an eternity before the narrow bit of rope braced against her instep. Slowly, she lowered her other foot and then her body until she'd totally committed herself again to what she feared might well prove to be the vehicle of her demise. One small consolation eased the threat of imminent disaster; at least the ladder wasn't swaying as it had on the journey upward.

Eerie stillness surrounded her as, one foot at a time she tentatively lowered herself down the sheer cliff, aching fingers clutching the abrasive lanyard. A soft whimpering invaded the silence, magnifying her anxiety, until she realized the sound came from her own frightened chest. Too late, rationality restored itself. Surely, she must be nearing the bottom rung by now. Where was the box stationed at the base of the ladder this morning? Her searching foot flailed in empty space. The tortured muscles of her arms cried out for mercy, her cold cramped fingers could no longer maintain their grip. She was about to release her hold, to chance what, at that point, she felt certain would be a fatal drop to the beach below when she felt strong hands encircling her waist, lifting her from her precarious perch. She gratefully welcomed the reassuring firmness of wet sand beneath her feet.

The security offered by the hands at her waist disappeared as quickly as it appeared. Marla whirled away from the rock wall, her frightful journey down the unstable ladder, and peered eagerly into the swirling mist for some glimpse of her rescuer. There was no doubt in her mind the hands offering her salvation belonged to the elusive sea captain.

"Captain Mallory?" Nebulous clouds of gray eddied about her, greedily swallowed her muffled cry, then closed in around her, holding her captive in their icy, dampness. Anxiety, then fear, became her only counsel. "Captain Mallory?" She heard the panic in her own voice. "Please, don't leave me. Jacob? Jacob!"

CHAPTER EIGHTEEN

She felt the firmness of his hand at her elbow, looked up toward the shadowy figure emerging from the mist. The fisherman's cap, resting low upon his forehead, failed to conceal dark eyes, softened now with concern. Marla was unable to suppress the ragged sigh of relief hiccuping past her lips.

"I --- I don't know the way back to the cottage," she offered shakily. "I --- I have a terrible time with direction."

"I suspect I know that." The captain acknowledged, his lips hovering on the edge of a smile. "Don't fret, Miss Mahla. I'll see to it you get home safe."

Startled, at first, by the sound of her name upon his lips, Marla found herself strangely comforted by the husky reassurance in his voice. Her earlier trepidation melted away. The opaque vapor shrouding the beach proved no more dense than her own inexplicable state of euphoric fog as, Jacob's hand never leaving her elbow, they navigated the all-too-short distance to Ed's place. Marla silently conceded to a sharp twinge of disappointment as the vague outline of the cottage loomed ahead.

"You'll be safe now, Miss. Mahla." The throaty voice whispered at her ear, paused, then, "It'd be best if you just stay away from the cabin."

Surprised at the sternness of the unexpected warning, a moment passed before Marla realized his hand no longer grasped her elbow. Though she turned quickly, her benefactor was already disappearing into the obliterating mist.

❦   ❦   ❦

Marla hastened to turn on the lights, not only to rid the cottage of its oppressive darkness, but also to hopefully dispel the strange, hollow, emptiness spreading inside her. The artificial illumination didn't help. A despairing loneliness settled like a heavy stone in the pit of her stomach. Restlessly, she wandered through the silent rooms, haunted by the memory of the gentle hand at her elbow, the quiet, yet insistent, warning. Stay away from the cabin? After today, she knew the improbable likelihood of her following that directive.

Gone, too, were any doubts she may have sheltered regarding the mortality of the lost captain of the Sea Nymph. Just as positive in her certainty he could not be Cape Cod ghost was her determination to somehow find a way to meet again with one Captain Jacob Mallory.

The muted rumble of an auto engine, the grating crunch of tires upon the graveled driveway, intruded upon Marla's introspection. A sudden beam of light flashed across the kitchen window. It took but an instant for Marla's mind to translate the implications. Elation scattered the disastrous thoughts corrupting her logic. Naomi and Reba were back from Boston! She was across the room and out the door before her friends had time to disembark from the front seat of the car.

"Naomi! Reba!" Marla enfolded first one, and then the other of her startled companions in an eager embrace. "You're home. I'm so glad you're here! I'm so glad to see you!"

The questioning frown flitting across Naomi's forehead warned Marla of her perhaps excessive display of exuberance. In an effort to recover her composure, she snatched a suitcase from the back seat and turned toward the cottage.

"I'm surprised you braved this terrible fog," Marla offered over her shoulder. "If I'd known you were coming in tonight, I'd have rustled up something for dinner, or at least brewed a pot of coffee."

"And just how were we supposed to contact you, by mental telepathy? You don't have a functioning cell phone, you know." Weariness sharpened an edge to Naomi's voice. "I can't believe you haven't replaced your cell phone battery by now."

"Neither can I, Naomi," Marla placated. "Honestly, I've tried. But I don't think this village even knows what a cell phone is. Nobody in town carries batteries. Talk about frustrating."

"Let me tell you about frustrating, as if the last two days weren't bad enough, then driving all afternoon in this blasted fog."

Marla glanced back at Reba who had retrieved the rest of the luggage. Her lips pursed in apology, she warned Marla into silence with a slight shake of her head.

Slipping the traveling case inside the bedroom door, Marla returned to where Naomi had collapsed onto the living room sofa. "Well, since I don't have any coffee made," she ventured, "how about a chilled glass of Vouvray instead?"

Naomi's frown softened and a smile tugged at the tightness around her lips. "I knew there was a reason I liked traveling with you, Marla."

❦   ❦   ❦

The rest of the evening was spent; each of the three women curled up in some position of relaxation, with an animated account of Naomi and Reba's misadventures in the metropolis of Boston. Since Naomi commandeered the couch, Reba settled into the overstuffed chair. Marla found her comfort ensconced in the nest of pillows strategically stacked upon the floor. Words wrestled for supremacy as both travelling companions sought to ensure not even the smallest traumatic detail was omitted.

"You'd think you'd be able to stop at a restaurant for lunch without having to worry about your car being stolen." Marla heard the rebirth of Naomi's exasperation, her voice rising as she recounted the felony. "Honestly, I still can't believe the audacity of the man. Broad daylight in a busy part of downtown, people walking by on the sidewalk, and he brazenly hot-wires our car and drives off."

Marla wanted to ask her if the car door had been left unlocked but decided it was likely not the best time to make such an inquiry. Instead, she offered the support of her own indignation.

"It just isn't safe anywhere, anymore," she commiserated. "In most cases, being able to contact the police relatively soon probably plays a big part in early apprehension."

A sharp glance from Reba reminded Marla she was supposedly not privy to Naomi's cell phone faux pas. "So, tell me," she hurried on. "Did you find out anything about him, his name, where lived, why he stole the car?"

Fortunately diverted from its disastrous course, the conversation moved on to a safer subject, the villainous carjacker. "I didn't ask and I couldn't care less." Naomi seemed to welcome the opportunity to renew her attack upon the scoundrel who'd irreverently sullied this, until then, perfect segment of her vacation. "They did say he was a drifter, a street person."

"According to the officer at the station, it isn't the first time this has happened," Reba embellished. " This guy steals cars then, instead of vamoosing out of town, just waits to get caught. He gets thrown in jail, and for awhile has someplace to sleep, plus three meals a day." Reba's voice grew soft. "I think that is so sad. I really feel sorry for him."

"Well, not me," came Naomi's testy response. "Oh, I'm sorry for his lot in life, but what infuriates me is if the police know about him, why don't they take him off the streets, or at least keep a closer eye on him. He totally ruined our visit to Boston."

"Oh, Naomi, that's not true," Reba disagreed. "Except for a few inconvenient hours, I had a wonderful time, and so did you. After all, it turned out okay in the end."

Marla could see the evening's camaraderie disintegrating. "What about your visit to Boston?" she quickly intervened. "I'm dying to hear all about the great historical treasures you uncovered."

Thus rerouted, the evening's "crash and burn" destiny was avoided and pleasantries restored. Marla's own thoughts were temporarily diverted from the enigma of a little gray cabin and an elusive sea captain, as she became lost in the delightful recounting of what had been a wonderful side trip for her co-travelers. The conscientious clock dutifully ticked its way into the night. It was nearly midnight before their chatter began to languish, and the lateness of the hour forced the three companions to reluctantly acknowledge a postponed day's-end weariness.

"It's certainly been an eventful vacation," Naomi sighed. "That much, I'll have to admit."

"I hate to see it end," Reba echoed.

"Well, all things, good and bad, do come to an end." Naomi rationalized. "Time to start packing. Tomorrow, it'll be back to the grind." Reaching for the purse still resting beside her on the couch, she dug into its mysterious innards to retrieve her cell phone. "I guess we'd better check to see which flights are open."

While Marla was familiar with this is customary procedure for agents flying standby, she found herself reluctant to initiate this necessary pre-flight query. The bevy of unanswered questions, held in abeyance during the evening's socializing, now charged back onto the battlefield of her vacillating rationale. How could she possibly leave before the mystery of Jacob Mallory was solved? But Naomi already held the phone pressed to her ear. Marla could hear her muted conversation with the reservation agent at the other end of the line.

"Well, that settles it," Naomi finally announced, closing the cover of her cell phone. "Delta's flights are pretty full until one forty-five in the afternoon so I guess I'll opt for that one. Reba, Northwest has a fairly open flight at two o'clock. Marla, looks like you're going to be stuck here until United's four o'clock departure, at best."

"No problem," Marla agreed. "That'll give me time to see you gals off before I turn in the rental car."

"Sure you don't mind?"

"Not at all," Marla insisted knowing the last place she wanted to be tomorrow afternoon was aboard that four o'clock flight back to Seattle.

CHAPTER NINETEEN

Naomi's flight turned out to be wide open, a lot of space available, but an uncomfortable half-hour passed at the Northwest gate before Reba was finally assured of a seat on the crowded flight back to Seattle. Marla waited until Reba disappeared down the loading ramp before, with a sigh of relief, she returned to the concourse leading back to the main terminal. She'd never gotten used to the white-knuckle uncertainty of flying standby. But she found if she put her mind on robot, she could remain sane until, eventually, passage was granted. Nerve wracking, she had to admit, but the price was right.

An escalator delivered her to Ground Transportation where she took her place in the line forming at the Hertz Rental Car booth. There were only two customers ahead of her, but to Marla's frustration, they both turned out to be problem clients; one didn't speak English, the other didn't like the car model assigned to him. She'd long since learned impatience only begot more impatience. So, Marla turned her thoughts to other things, like, what else, Jacob Mallory, the deserted beach cabin and the reluctant resignation to never knowing the answers to that mystery.

An irascible idea tiptoed into her meandering thoughts. What would happen, it suggested, if she didn't catch that flight to Seattle, if she stayed here at Cape Cod for a few more days? Marla shrugged it off as a totally irrational, absolutely impossible concept. How would she ever explain her actions to Naomi and Reba? However, once tempted, her challenged imagination refused to be so easily silenced. "*Tell them the United flights were full,*" it whispered, "*that you couldn't get out of Boston today. They know the uncertainties of flying on standby.*"

"*But that would only work for one day,*" argued her common sense. "*They know you're due back at your desk at the travel agency by Monday, just the day after tomorrow.*"

Oh, lordy! Her reasoning, totally out of control now, spewed forth a list of options. She could call her supervisor, maybe she pull some of her sick leave time. But then, there was the problem of accommodations. Where would she stay? She didn't recall having seen any motels in or near the village. The cottage where they'd spent the past two weeks came to mind. Would she dare go back there? The key should still be under the doormat where they'd left it. Marla disliked taking advantage of Naomi's brother, but still . . . Ed's place would probably be the best place, especially if she wanted to be near the fishing village . . . and the cabin. She would explain it all to Naomi when she called her, which, however, she couldn't see herself having the courage to do for at least several days. But why was she stewing about it, anyway? The whole idea was ludicrous.

Half an hour passed before Naomi finally found herself smiling across the counter at the harried Hertz rental agent. "Hi." Offering her a solicitous grimace of compassion, Marla slid her paperwork across the counter. "Looks like you're having a pretty tough day."

The young woman behind the counter glanced down at Marla's travel agent identification and her polite customer-greeting smile fading, she rolled her eyes toward the ceiling. "Honestly," she sighed. "Can you believe some people?'

"Can I believe people can be like that, no," Marla commiserated. "Do I believe there are people like that, yes, I get my share every day."

"Oh, well, you know all about it, then," the agent sympathized picking up the rental contract Marla filled out only two weeks before. "You turning your car in?"

Marla hesitated for one fateful moment while common sense struggled with irrationality. "Well, actually," she heard herself saying, "I'd like to extend my rental."

A frown flitted across the rental agent's forehead. "Did you call in a reservation?"

"No, I'm sorry," Marla explained at the questioning lift of eyebrows. "I didn't know until this morning I'd be needing the car longer. If there's a problem, I understand."

The young woman's fingers danced across the keys of her computer while the line between her eyebrows deepened. The frown disappeared, the smile returned. "No problem."

She scribbled a new date on the paperwork in front of her then slid it back across the counter. "I've booked you for another two weeks. Just be sure to call if you need longer."

Marla released the breath she hadn't realized she held trapped in her throat. The decision had been made for her.

"Oh, great," she stammered. "Great. Thanks, thanks a lot. I really appreciate this."

Clutching the revised contract in her hand, Marla turned back into the terminal. *Oh lordy.* What had she done? Whatever was she going to say to Naomi, to Reba, to her supervisor? Well, that's something she'd just have to worry about later. For now, she needed to decide where she was going to stay for the next fourteen days.

Marla stopped at an electronics kiosk on her way out of the building to pick up a new battery for her cell phone, plus an extra, just in case, and headed for the parking lot.

🍁   🍁   🍁

CHAPTER TWENTY

Feeling every bit the trespasser, Marla lifted the doormat and retrieved the key to the cottage left there a few hours earlier. Indecision still nibbled at her conscience, and it was a moment before she slipped the notched bit of metal into the lock. Then, surrendering to what she decided must surely be the dictates of Karma, she pushed aside her guilt, and lifting her suitcase from the stoop, stepped into the quiet confines of the little kitchen. The ambience of the room with all its culinary potential reminded her she'd not eaten since breakfast. However, all perishable food had been tossed out before they left. The by now tiresome choice offered by the remaining can of Dinty Moore stew did little to stimulate her appetite. There appeared to be enough coffee for the next morning, but as for dinner, well, talk about deja vu. Just as on the first night of her vacation, prospects for an evening meal appeared to be no more than the fresh apple tucked into her purse earlier in the day.

❧　　❧　　❧

The morning's second cup of very strong coffee helped abate the gnawing emptiness in her stomach, but did little to appease the banshees of guilt howling at the gates of her conscience. Marla knew she must call Naomi, the item topping her list of things to do that day. A call to her supervisor loomed as a very strong second. Still, the food supply needed to be replenished if she was to survive for two more weeks. Perhaps she should do that first, she reasoned. A hopeful search of the pantry revealed nothing more than that lone can of Dinty Moore's beef stew plus two red and white labeled cans of Campbell's cream of tomato soup. Neither quite filled her concept of a suitable morning meal.

An impassioned hunger dredged up the memory of a previous breakfast, and the image of Mo's diner, that charming little restaurant situated on the Village Square, flickered across her mind. An order of Mo's cranberry muffins slathered with vodka-laced blueberry jam sounded mighty enticing about now. Marla slipped into her parka, snatched her purse from the counter. She would call Naomi later. Besides, she really needed time to decide how to break the news of this, her latest, and probably most hair-brained of escapades.

She hesitated on the doorstep, pondering whether to walk to the village or take the car. The sky was clear, the sun - warm. A gentle breeze drifting from the bay carried with it the pungent sea odor of iodine and stranded kelp. Marla decided the stroll would do her good. She closed the door firmly, and, as was her habit when Reba, Naomi and she were going different directions, slipped the key beneath the mat.

❦   ❦   ❦

The meal surpassed all her expectations, the muffins sumptuous, the blueberry jam heady. Her carnal needs satisfied Marla now turned her attention to more pressing issues, the first and most important being the call to Naomi. Procrastination tempted her. She did need to call her supervisor. Perhaps she should make that call first. Frustration forced a sigh from her lips. There was no easy way out. Apprehension would ride on her shoulders until she faced the unpleasantness of the call to Naomi. But not here, she cringed: not the café where attentive ears of the village could bear witness to her vacuous depravity.

Marla glanced across the room to where the buxom, middle-aged waitress originally introducing her to vodka-laced blueberry jam, stood beside the museum-worthy cash register. The bodice of a faded pink uniform, worn thin from numerous washings, stretched tightly across the woman's ample bosom. Tiny plastic buttons clung precariously to frayed edges of disintegrating buttonholes. Bright pink shell earrings dangled below fiery, hennaed hair. Her thick arms resting upon the counter, the waitress studied Marla with unguarded curiosity. Marla returned the scrutiny with a cordial smile.

"Those muffins were absolutely delicious," she enthused. Suspecting she'd no doubt be frequenting this restaurant in the coming days, Marla felt the need to court at least one friendly face in this hostile village. "I can hardly wait to sample your lunch menu."

The contemplation tensing the food server's fleshy features slowly relaxed into a grin. "You best be early if you wanna get heah before it's gone," she admonished. "We're having lobstah chowdah today."

"I'll definitely plan on an early lunch," Marla promised. Counting out the amount to cover the cost of her breakfast, she made sure to include a generous tip. "Reserve a bowl of that chowder for me, will you?" she offered with an invitational arch of her eyebrows. "My name's Marla."

The waitress glanced down at the bills Marla slid across the counter and her cherry red lips curved into a smile. " I can do that . . . Mahla," she nodded, stuffing the tip money into her apron pocket. "If I'm out in the kitchen, you just ask for Ruthie. That's me."

Stepping out onto the street, Marla looked about for a spot affording at least a small amount of privacy when she faced her moment of truth. Acceptance of a small bench in front of the museum satisfied her search.

Anticipating Naomi's reaction, Marla probed her innermost psyche for some approach to justify her actions. Hadn't she heard somewhere the best defense was a good offense? In this case, and considering her companion's uncanny perception of the truth, she wasn't sure what a good offense might be. With a sigh of resignation, she decided just to throw herself upon the mercy of their friendship and fumbled for the communication device tucked in the pocket of her parka.

Crowding aside the pleasantness of her recent repast, a cold lump of uneasiness settled itself in the pit of Marla's stomach. She listened to the muted summons of her cell phone reaching out into cyberspace, dreading the moment its persistent vibration would connect her with her friend.

"Marla!" Naomi's voice, sharp, excited, exploded into Marla's ear. "We've been worried sick about you. Thank goodness, you finally have your cell phone working. We've been trying to call. We had no idea you'd have to wait so long for space available. We could have taken later flights." She paused long enough to catch her breath, then added, "What time did you finally get out of Boston?"

Unformed words of response remained frozen on the back of Marla's tongue.

"Marla, you there?"

"Yes, yes, I'm here". She scarcely recognized the anemic sound escaping her numb lips. "The fact is . . .. " The words struggled through the constriction of her throat. "The fact is, I haven't left Boston. I'm still here, at Ed's cottage."

Now it was Marla's turn to challenge the silence. "Naomi, you there? Did you hear me? Look, I'm sorry about Ed's cottage. I shouldn't have come here. I'll start looking for a motel tomorrow."

Naomi's voice, an almost inaudible whisper, crept across space. "Why?"

" I don't want to impose upon your brother or take advantage of our friendship, Naomi. I'm sure I can find accommodations somewhere near here."

"No," Naomi, her voice stronger, interrupted. "Why didn't you catch the flight out of Boston? Why are you still in Cape Cod? What is it, Marla? Tell me, what's going on?"

"It's just, well, I don't know how to explain it, it's . . .."

"It's that cabin, isn't it?" Her perception didn't surprise Marla.

"There is something very strange going on, Naomi. I have to find out what it is."

"Are you out of your mind? It's none of our business what goes on down there. You could lose your job. Forget this nonsense. Come on home."

"I'm sorry, Naomi. I can't leave here, not yet."

The chasm of silence between them widened.

"Very well," The iciness of Naomi's response bade ill for their friendship. "I'll let Ed know someone is still using the cottage. I'm not sure of his plans but I'll ask him to let us know before he returns to the Cape."

"That isn't necessary. I can find another place to stay," Marla insisted. But her words were lost in space. The connection had been broken.

CHAPTER TWENTY-ONE

The bitter taste of remorse clung to Marla's tongue. She'd jeopardized a friendship that had endured for years. Maybe Naomi was right, maybe she was losing her mind. What went on in this little Cape Cod village really was none of her business. But then, she'd not been totally honest with her friend; hadn't shared the real reason she didn't board the plane back to Seattle. Memories of the concern mirrored in a pair of dark brooding eyes, the strong hand at her elbow, slipped across her mind. Until now, she hadn't admitted even to herself, it was much more than the mystery of an abandoned cabin keeping her in Cape Cod . . . much more.

The conversation with her supervisor, though not necessarily uplifting, proved at least a bit less stressful. While not exactly thrilled over such short notice at Marla's request for an extended vacation, the overseer ultimately surrendered to acceptance of Marla's "not feeling too well, must have picked up an East Coast bug" excuse and caved in to a plea for two weeks sick leave. Marla wasn't sure if she should be pleased or dismayed by this reinforcement of her debauchery, but the web grew tighter and there was no choice but to move forward.

In an effort to salve the discomfort of a smarting conscience, so recklessly hurtling itself into dereliction, Marla decided it best to find someplace other than Ed's cottage from which to launch her planned invasion into the privacy of the village. Obviously, the best place to begin her intrusive probing would be from within the village itself. But where did she look for those seemingly non-existent accommodations? An image of the stout figured waitress she'd just left drifted across her mind. Who else would have a better knowledge of the inner activities of the village?

Marla questioned whether returning to the café after such a short time might not seem a little premature, possibly arousing antennas of suspicion best left at rest. That left her with little choice but to idle away the balance of the morning. She resisted an urge to revisit the museum, strolling instead along the waterfront among decaying wooden docks, stained white by years of seagull tenancy. It didn't surprise her to discover a small pub, tucked in among the weathered buildings of the marina. She'd have been more surprised had there been no hideaway where sailors could ease their weariness at day's end. Evoking a smile from her was the discovery this particular little establishment called itself the Blue Crab, the tired placard in its fly specked window inviting all who would to "drop in and do the Blue Crab Boogie." Recalling Reba's recent discourse on the subject, Marla chose not to even speculate on what that might involve.

A small craft hugging the pier tugged at its moorage, the shattered mast sprawling across its gunnels, leaving little question as to the vessel's seaworthiness. For Marla, there was a haunting sadness about the disabled boat; something akin to an injured animal left behind. She moved forward to where faded letters across the bow identified the unfortunate *Marcie Dee*. Something familiar about the name jostled Marla's memory. Then she remembered, on the museum wall, one of the fishermen lost at sea had been captain of the *Marcie Dee*.

Quickly scanning the empty marina, Marla found herself wondering whatever had become of the Sea Nymph? Was she too, like her captain, presumably lost at sea? Or was she tied up somewhere, waiting to be restored, waiting for a new captain? Surely there must be some accounting, an article in the local newspaper. Assuming this little community even published a newspaper, Marla speculated as to where she might access old copies? It couldn't have been more than five or six months since the tragedy if her calculations were correct. But when efforts to recall a library or newspaper office in the village proved futile, Marla faced abandonment of any further research, until the image of the little bookstore crowded into her mind. She decided it was worth a try.

The Square appeared devoid now of fishermen and their nets. Anticipation buoyed her steps as Marla hastened across the worn stones.

She was relieved to discover the bookstore open. The overwhelming mustiness of old books greeted her at the door; the interior dimness challenged her mission. Slow in adjusting from the outside brightness, her eyes probed the murky light for some sign of the storekeeper.

A twig of a man, thin wisps of graying hair clinging valiantly to his pale scalp, stepped from behind a shelter of shopworn volumes stacked upon a table at the rear of the store. Smudged spectacles with one ear-piece missing balanced themselves upon the narrow bridge of his nose. Shoulders stooped as if he'd carried too many armloads of the heavy tomes, he scurried toward Marla, his hop-skip gait reminding her of an injured seagull.

"Good morning," she offered, with what she hoped was her most charming smile.

"Yes, yes, good morning, good morning," the shopkeeper bobbed his head impatiently. "Can I help you?"

"I certainly hope so," Marla hurried on. "I'm trying to find information regarding a fishing boat tragedy that may have been reported in one of the local newspapers. Would you, by chance, carry any of those earlier publications, say, for within the past six months?"

The little man halted midway between a hop and a skip. Recognition brought a startled frown to his forehead, dislodging his eyeglasses from their precarious perch. His hand fluttered nervously upward, intercepting their errant flight down the slender ridge of his nose. It was apparent Marla's visit upset him. Several uncomfortable moments passed before he responded, and then, only with a shrug of indifference and a vague gesture toward the far wall. Turning quickly, he hop-skipped back to the security of his book fortress, leaving Marla to continue on her own.

Following the storekeeper's irresolute directions, Marla worked her way through a maze of crowded bookshelves to a nearly obscure display rack clinging to the cluttered wall, thin sheaths of newsprint draped across its metal rods. Sifting through her memory, Marla struggled to recall the date posted below museum photo, the month of the supposed big storm and Captain Mallory's disappearance. Riffling through the slender sheets of press releases, she selected a publication bearing the date of this past March 18th. Disappointment rewarded her careful perusal of its few pages. She was about to return it to its rack when a small article boxed at the bottom of the back page, snagged her attention.

FIRE DESTROYS FISHING VESSEL.

Her eyes eagerly consumed the few lines that followed.

While on a recent fishing expedition, a fire of undetermined origin severely damaged the fishing vessel, Sea Nymph. Nearby boats responding to the scene of the disaster, reportedly were unable to locate its captain, Jacob Mallory who is presumed to have drowned.

A fire? Marla was certain the caption beneath the museum photo indicated the Sea Nymph disappeared during a storm. And hadn't Phil, the garage mechanic, inferred the same? How could Captain Mallory possibly have survived a fire at sea? Unless . . . the image of the Sea Nymph's seemingly abandoned skiff, resting on the sands below the cabin, reincarnated itself. Excitement stirred the hairs at the nape of her neck, quickened her heartbeat as Marla teetered on what she was sure was the edge of discovery. But before she could act upon her suspicions, she knew she must first find a place to stay.

❧   ❧   ❧

CHAPTER TWENTY-TWO

It was eleven thirty before Marla felt comfortable returning to the café. In spite of her ulterior motives, she found herself really anticipating that touted bowl of lobster chowder. The dining room, empty a few hours ago, now accommodated people in numbers she'd not witnessed during her morning stroll. Older fishermen, beached by age, who now spent their days lounging about the docks; the museum's curator, looking aloof and unapproachable at her table for one; a colorful assortment of stoic locals, shopkeepers Marla guessed, now filled the small room. If anyone even noticed her entrance, they chose to ignore it.

Over the heads of this chattering assemblage, Ruthie beamed at her, motioning her toward a little corner table. Marla hadn't realized how hungry she was, not only for the lobster chowder, but also for the sight of a friendly face in this hostile village. Making her way across the room, she no sooner seated herself before Ruthie was placing a bowl of steaming soup in front of her.

"Just like I promised, Hon," she whispered patting Marla's shoulder. "Wouldn't want it gettin' around, though." Marla was startled by the slightly caustic edge to Ruthie's voice. "These folks don't take kindly to sharin' with outsiders, especially when it comes to our lobstah chowdah."

That's not all they don't take kindly to, Marla wanted to retort. Instead, she smiled her gratitude. "Thanks," she whispered back. "It'll be our secret."

Marla finished the ambrosia before her and concluded that she, herself, would be reluctant to share knowledge of such a delectable concoction were it her secret. Dawdling over her coffee, she ordered a second cup, waiting for the room to empty. She hovered on the edge of an oncoming set of coffee nerves before the last of the lunch-goers scraped the final spoonful from his bowl, pushed back his chair and, after a short, friendly exchange with Ruthie about the local weather, ambled from the café. But for the unseen employee clattering dishes in the kitchen, Marla was left alone with her intended confidante.

She waited while the plates from the departing customer were collected, waited while Ruthie, returning from the kitchen, swiped a damp towel across the vacated table. Towel in hand, Ruthie turned, and while her smile was friendly, Marla suspected the waitress was assessing the anticipated length of her stay.

"More coffee, Hon?" Ruthie offered, although the tone of her voice suggested it was time for Marla to surrender her cup.

Ignoring the obvious inference and, turning her back on caution, Marla launched herself into the unknown territory of her plan. "I suppose I've had enough," she acquiesced. "I can only put off facing my problem for so long." Marla let a sigh slip from her lips. "You've been so nice, Ruthie. Thanks, again, for saving the chowder for me. It really was delicious. I can see why your people are so reluctant to share it with outsiders."

As she had hoped, curiosity snared her prey. White towel clutched in her hand like flag of truce, the victim aborted her journey toward the kitchen. Crossing the distance between them, she plopped into the chair opposite Marla.

"Huh, don't call these hard-headed bluenoses my people," she groused. "I ain't even from around here."

"Oh?" Now Marla's curiosity was peaked. "Don't you live here in the village?"

With a wave of her hand Ruthie dismissed the question as if brushing away a pesky fly. "I only work here."

Lordy, does everyone in this town harbor a secret, Marla wondered?

Resting her supple arms upon the table, Ruthie leaned toward Marla, her face tight with concern. "You got a problem, Honey? Nothin' too serious, I hope."

Marla carefully studied the dark dregs coating the bottom of her coffee cup. "Well, I suppose not." She offered another weary sigh. "Except, of course, to me. I have to find a place to stay tonight."

Marla's confessor reared back in her chair, her expression one of disbelief. "I thought you was stayin' at Ed's place."

"Ed is my friend's brother," Marla explained. "I don't really feel comfortable staying there now that she's gone back to Seattle."

"Well, there ain't many places for tourists around here, most folks bein' fishermen. Except for people like Ed, we don't see many strangers in these parts." Ruthie's brow furrowed as she weighed the problem she opted to take on as her own. "Let me see, now." She paused, fixing a thoughtful gaze upon the steam-yellowed ceiling overhead. "Oh, yes." Her eyes, brightening with recollection met Marla's. "There's Mrs. Doolittle's boardin' house on Sand Dune Drive. Ain't much more than a rickety old two story building but she does let out rooms to some of the fishermen."

Encouraged by this willingness to help, a sudden impulse fluttered into Marla's thoughts. Reluctantly, she forced herself to swallow the urge crowding to her lips; an urge to ask Ruthie what she knew about Jacob Mallory. Judging from the reactions received in the past, Marla feared that question might very possibly sabotage the fragile structure of this new, uncertain relationship. She found herself unwilling to take that chance. With directions sketched upon the paper napkin clutched in her hand, Marla bid farewell to her benefactor and set out for Sand Dune Drive.

CHAPTER TWENTY THREE

Following Ruthie's directions, it was an easy walk to the far end of the village where, as promised, a faded street sign identified a barely discernable roadway as Sand Dune Drive. The rutted street, climbing up a sandy knoll, provided access to but one residence. Surrounded by a sea of beach grass, abused by sun and salty sea air, a dilapidated two-story building perched atop the hillock, like an old lady of the mountain, rising in haughty disdain above the humble shacks crouching at her feet. Barely visible from the road, a sun-bleached, water-stained placard propped inside the front window seemed almost reluctant in its declaration "Rooms to Let."

The short hike up to the formidable looking structure proved more difficult than the longer trek from the café, leaving Marla more than a little winded by the time she stepped onto the sagging front porch. Pausing a moment to catch her breath, she lifted her curled fingers toward the weathered oaken door. But before she could tap upon the sand-scarred panel, it opened and Marla was staring into the scowling countenance of a middle-aged woman she assumed to be her potential landlady.

Wisps of gray-streaked hair, escaping from an untidy dark brown bun clinging precariously to the nape of her neck, framed the woman's pale, hostile features. Wiping her hands upon the flour-dusted apron girding her mature figure, she glared at Marla through dark, narrowed eyes.

"What're you doing here?" Her demand was delivered through tight, bloodless lips. "What do you want?"

Although it was becoming an all-too-familiar greeting in this unfriendly village, Marla was startled by this unprovoked display of animosity. "I . . . I'm looking for a room to rent," she stammered. "At the café . . ." She hesitated, alerted by her subconscious that giving Ruthie as reference might not be to her new friend's best interest. "At the café where I had breakfast this morning," she continued cautiously, "I overheard someone mention you rent out rooms."

The response was curt. "Ain't got none left. They're all rented."

"But your sign . . ." Marla motioned toward the contradictory placard filling the corner of the window.

"I said, they're all rented!"

A hiss of anger still hanging in the air, the hostile face disappeared and Marla found herself staring at an equally unfriendly oaken door panel.

"Must be the heavy summer tourist season," she muttered.

Her sarcasm was stifled as a curtain fluttered in the window and the incriminating "Room to Let" sign was rudely snatched from its post. Smarting from this blatant display of undisguised rejection, Marla glared her disapproval at the sorry-looking structure: ugly with its peeling paint, chipped cornices, unwashed second-story windows.

What benefit is a view Marla bristled, *if you can't see out of the windows?* Her belligerent gaze razed the face of the ancient building when a movement in the window directly above her brought her critical perusal to a halt. Someone was standing at an upstairs window, watching her. Even across the distance between them, even despite the smudged windowpane, she recognized those tanned, scowling features.

Adonis!

Uneasiness guided her steps from the rotting porch, stirred the hairs at the nape of her neck as Marla forced herself to slowly retrace the seemingly endless distance across the sandy knoll, aware those dark eyes followed each step of her retreat. Thus intimidated, her good judgement resurfaced. Perhaps it would be best, she decided, if she were to return to the cottage where she could reorganize, maybe even reconsider her plans for alternate accommodations. After all, Naomi did say she could stay at Ed's place. Of course, her friend had also questioned her sanity. At this uneasy point in time, Marla was beginning to think Naomi might be right about the latter.

Her mind a maelstrom of indecision, Marla worked her way back through the narrow streets of the village, while each unresolved, tormenting doubt churned within the whirlpool of her confusion. What did she expect to prove by staying in Cape Cod? Perhaps she'd never see Jacob Mallory again. At the thought, a strange hollowness filled the pit of her stomach. Hadn't he, himself, warned her, urged her to go back home? Yet, would her life ever return to any semblance of normalcy until she found answers to the mystery plaguing her during these past two weeks? But foremost in her mind, having jeopardized her friendship with Naomi, could she, in good conscious, remain at Ed's cottage?

So pre-occupied with her dilemma, scarcely aware of the passage of time and distance, Marla was actually startled to glance up and discover the cottage; the rental car parked in the driveway, only a few yards away. Still immersed in her irresolution, she skirted the vehicle to the walkway beyond. She'd gone but a few steps before she caught sight of a familiar object resting upon the porch . . . her suitcase. It was lying upon her bed, open and partially unpacked, when she left for breakfast this morning.

Her earlier anxiety forgotten, she hastened across the uneven cobblestones to where her suitcase now sat, closed and tightly zipped, upon the cottage doorstep. A few aggressive twists of the doorknob left no doubt; the door was still locked. Stooping, she reached beneath the doormat, but her groping fingers were rewarded with no more than a gritty mound of sand. Frantically, she snatched the mat from its assignment, thereby removing any possible doubt. The key, stashed there earlier, was gone.

Marla's mind was immediately awash with an entirely new set of problems. What on earth was going on? Who would have entered the cottage in her absence, removed her belongings, absconded with the key? His image suddenly flashed across her mind: Jeremiah. The cottage caretaker, arbitrarily appointing himself her evictor, left no doubt as to the intent of his actions.

The indecisiveness commandeering her thoughts but a few moments ago quickly dissolved, replaced by smoldering indignation. The audacity of the man, how dare he, without so much as a "by your leave," take it upon himself to dictate her decisions? The bubbling lava of anger spilled across her rationale, smothering all remnants of reasoning. *That settled it!* There was no way she was leaving the Cape now. Jeremiah, the curator, the landlady, the entire village --- they'd find she was not so easily intimidated.

In response to a timid emissary of logic tapping at her subconscious, she opened the door to a troublesome reality. She had no place to stay. With the cottage no longer a possibility, nor Mrs. Doolittle's "Rooms to Let," where did that leave her tonight? Either sleeping on the beach, she speculated, or in the limited accommodations of the rental car, neither option particularly appealing. Where, then? That erratic butterfly of irrationality flitted once again past the window of her judgement. *The cabin . . . what about Jacob's cabin?*

"Well, why not?" came the irrational response to the horrified reaction of her practical self. "The place is supposedly abandoned and even if Jeremiah should object, well, he's the one who locked me out of the cottage."

Marla closed her ears to whispered reprimands from a reproachful conscience, suggesting perhaps there was another, less logical motivation encouraging her return to the harbinger of her undoing.

CHAPTER TWENTY-FOUR

The sun was nearing completion of its journey across the afternoon sky when Marla turned off the highway onto the dusty road leading to the missing fisherman's cabin. Fortunately, remaining remnants of her fractured common sense reminded her there was likely no food at the cabin. If she persisted in the presumption she would be residing at that isolated habitat, she needed to shop. At the tiny market outside of town, she made a hurried selection of basic, quick-to-fix necessities. Belated recollection of the little wood-burning kitchen stove, her only means of food preparation, dictated her choice of coffee, sweet rolls, lunch meats and an assortment of easy heat-and-eat canned goods which, of course, included the ever reliable Dinty Moore's beef stew. *Lordy*, how she did miss the convenience of the microwave sitting back in her Seattle apartment.

Pulling the Hertz rental into the wide spot at the foot of the path, Marla turned off the key, silencing the throbbing engine. In the sudden absence of its sound, she heard only the moaning of the wind, mourning the futility of its efforts as it flung itself against the uncompromising indifference of a craggy bluff. An uneasy reluctance slowed her steps as she climbed from the car. The gray-sided building looming above seemed to reflect the hostility she'd just witnessed in the village. For a moment, her determination wavered and she toyed with a temptation to reconsider her earlier decision.

Further threatening her resolve was the sight of the rutted pathway leading up the embankment. She'd failed to consider her earlier ascent up that formidable five-hundred foot slope, pulling her luggage behind her, a journey to be twice repeated today if she hoped to transfer the supplies filling the trunk of the Hertz rental up to the cabin. Well, it wouldn't be the first time she'd faced such intimidating circumstances, she reminded herself. Dragging cumbersome baggage through Europe with its inadequate bus service; its lack of elevator service to third floor accommodations, prepared her for nearly any challenge. Contemplating the climb now facing her, she was grateful for experience teaching her to pack light.

Marla hesitated while the fine line between good judgement and misdirected commitment dissolved before a wave of irrational stubbornness and determination. Taking a deep breath for courage, she yanked open the lid to the car's trunk. First, she wrestled her luggage to the ground, then scooped up the sack of provisions so necessary for her survival. Balancing the flimsy paper bag on her hip with one hand, Marla wrapped the fingers of her other hand about the handle of the wheeled suitcase and began the arduous journey upward.

Her lungs ached with the merciless labor of breathing; her trembling knees threatened to buckle beneath her while her numbed arms were devoid of any feeling at all. Ignoring the quivering bundle of pain that was her body, she paused before the cabin door. The contents of the unwieldy sack on her hip had shifted with one rebellious can of stew now seeking escape through an opportune rend in inferior paper. Allowing herself only a moment's hesitation, lest her courage and determination totally desert her, she transferred her cramped hand from the luggage handle to the shiny black doorknob. A nervous breath of relief sighed past her lips as the door, responding to pressure, obligingly swung inward. Relieved, she dismissed the fear lurking in the back of her mind that perhaps Jeremiah, anticipating her move might also have barred access to the cabin.

Reclaiming its handle, Marla forced the battered wheels of her suitcase across the marred thresh hold and stepped once again into the familiar dimly lit interior. Gratefully depositing the rapidly disintegrating grocery bag onto the counter, she hastened to the window and pulled back the hopsacking draperies. No longer held at bay, the afternoon sun invaded the room. It was as she remembered it: the wood stove glared coldly from its station against the wall, the spindly-legged table with its two cane-backed chairs stood in rigid readiness. Despite this austere reception, Marla experienced a feeling of excitement, anticipation; an expectation she felt reluctant to acknowledge, yet could no longer deny. Here, at Jacob Mallory's cabin, where she'd encountered him once before, she felt certain would be the most probable place to once again encounter him face to face.

Meanwhile, she faced the chore of settling in. Closeting of her meager supply of provisions in the cabinet above the stove was accomplished in short order. Trundling her dust-covered suitcase into the bedroom she dispatched the task of hanging her few items of clothing within an equally short period of time. Now she confronted the question of what to do with the rest of her time until . . . until what, she asked herself? Just exactly what did she expect would happen, Jacob Mallory appearing on cue? Once again she was revisited by restless gremlins of doubt, their whispered accusations of imprudence reinforced by the echo of Naomi's last comment, "Are you out of your mind?"

No! She refused to be intimidated by such negativism. Whether influenced by head or heart, she would not be dissuaded from her earlier decision. Marla snatched her parka from its hook beside the door. Maybe a little fresh air would clear her head.

Once outside, Marla contemplated the choice of strolling about the limited confines of the mesa or, even more to her liking, taking a stroll on the beach. In her present state of mind, the ship's ladder held little appeal. That left the option of getting into the car and driving to a beach access. She was reluctant to abandon her hard-won bastion, yet a sudden craving for the camaraderie of human contact overwhelmed her. She decided instead to visit Mo's Shanty, check out the dinner menu; maybe even enjoy a chat with her new friend.

❦　　　❦　　　❦

The trip to the village by car seemed relatively short to Marla compared to the much longer journey the day she'd been forced to traverse it on foot --- when was it, only two weeks ago? So much had happened; an eternity seemed to have passed. She parked the car in the lot reserved for museum attendants and walked the short distance to the café. The eatery seemed oddly empty for what Marla would have supposed to be the dinner hour. But then, she conceded, perhaps eating habits of Cape Cod fishermen varied from those of Seattle travel agents. She chose a seat at the counter, assuming it would provide more of an opportunity to visit unobtrusively with Ruthie than if she were seated at one of the tables.

She was surprised, and more than a little disappointed, when the pink-uniformed waitress finally emerging from the back room was not Ruthie. But, of course, Marla rationalized, if Ruthie had the morning shift, she wouldn't be there to serve the dinner trade. Marla hadn't thought of that before she left the mesa. She smiled at the too-thin older woman behind the counter whose face seemed set in an eternal expression of disapproval. Marla received no reaction to her friendly gesture.

"You gonna order?" was the curt demand.

"Ah – well, maybe a cup of coffee, I guess." Marla ignored the splash of dark, steaming liquid sloshing onto the counter as the ceramic mug was rudely plunked in front of her. She plucked the plastic covered menu from its station beside the napkin holder, and after a quick perusal of its food-spattered list of entrees, decided to try again.

"I had some of your delicious lobster chowder for lunch," she ventured. "It was absolutely out of this world. Do you have any left?"

Neither compliment nor inquiry evoked a response. The ill-tempered waitress continued to ignore Marla, busying herself with the creation of a fresh pot of coffee. It was apparent to Marla her presence was not welcome. Obviously, she'd not be dining at Mo's tonight.

"Ah . . . pardon me, ma'am . . . the other waitress, Ruthie, what time does she come on shift tomorrow?"

"She don't work heah no more." The information was offered tersely and without explanation.

"But . . . what . . . why . . . this afternoon . . . .." Marla was left to her own confused assumptions as, with a glowering glance in Marla's direction, the uncompromising food server disappeared into the kitchen.

❦   ❦   ❦

Back on the mesa, Marla settled herself onto the sparse grass covering the lip of the bluff; gazed out across the bay, hoping the soothing undulation of its waters would massage away the torture of confusion. Had Ruthie lost her job? It certainly didn't seem believable her friend would quit with such short notice. Was it her meddling,

Marla agonized, causing so much trouble for others? She was beginning to have serious doubts about her own good judgement, or perhaps more aptly, the lack thereof.

The sun was dipping into the waters of the bay when Marla finally rose from her sea watch and returned to the cabin. Creating a fire in the small cook stove turned out to be less of a challenge than she'd expected, and before long, a tantalizing pot of stew, ala Dinty Moore, bubbled atop the metal surface. Unassuming as it might be, the meal, enhanced by the pride of achievement, was a satisfying one.

The cleanup proved a little less pleasurable since water to wash the dishes also needed to be heated atop the stove. Contents of the wood box, once so plentifully stocked, were being quickly depleted and Marl foresaw a chilly night ahead of her. Uneasily aware of its overhead attic access, she entertained no intention of making use of the bedroom facilities. Besides, she did not wish to retire this early.

Carefully closing the hopsacking against the enigma of night's approaching darkness, Marla wrapped herself in the blanket she'd retrieved from the foot of the bed. A wry speculation of the sleeping arrangements she'd endured during this vacation reminded her, sans the comforts of a bed, many nights found her, wrapped in whatever blanket available, curled up on various and sundry pieces of furniture. Flicking on the lamp, she tucked her feet beneath her, opened her copy of *Runaway to Tahiti* and waited for the night to overtake her.

Marla was deeply engrossed in the misadventures of the Tahiti-bound couple when a sound outside diverted her attention; a scuffle on the pathway gravel, a shuffling sound on the door stoop. She listened into the silence, hoping to identify the interruption. There was nothing but the distant thunder of the eternal waves, doggedly bombarding the sandy beach. Then, she heard it again, a movement, just outside the cabin door. Paralyzed, she watched its black knob slowly turn. Her heart lost cadence, fluttered weakly then, as if seeking escape, beat wildly within her chest. Jacob? Fear and hope, anticipation and dread, each vying for dominance, elbowed their way into the dryness of her constricted throat. Would he be angry? Or would compassion and concern soften those brooding features?

Untangling herself from the restricting blanket, Marla lowered her feet to the floor where *Tahiti* now lay forgotten. Rising from the couch, she'd taken but one hesitant step toward the entryway when the door suddenly swung inward. Framed in the opening was the tall, muscular figure of a seaman, an all-too-familiar tee-shirted figure. Only now the bold, flashing smile was gone from the dark, tanned face; there was no flirtatious twinkle in the eyes of the fisherman she and her friends once dubbed "Adonis."

CHAPTER TWENTY-FIVE

Reflexes seemed to momentarily fail her, then suddenly rally. Marla didn't wait for an explanation from the intruder, his unexpected appearance leaving little doubt in her mind but that his intentions were lecherous. Her reactivated endorphin system telegraphed its frantic message; *escape, you must escape.* The only exit blocked, she flung herself across the room and into the bedroom. Responding to the survival commands of a primal subconscious, Marla slammed the door behind her and reached for the rope releasing the stairway to the attic.

Even as her searching foot connected with the bottom step of the slowly unfolding ladder, Marla was vaguely aware the stairway now blocked the door to the bedroom. Grateful for this bit of respite, she clambered up the narrow treads, scrambled over the once intimidating passage across the ceiling joists to the small window at the end of the gabled space. Her mind registered but sought no explanation as to why the window stood open; accepted only the fact it offered her an avenue of escape. Fear and necessity erased an earlier mistrust of the narrow slabs of wood descending the outside wall of the cabin. The sound of a human battering ram, slamming against the bedroom door, spurred her on.

Turning her back to the open window, Marla probed the night air with her foot until it settled onto the first slender strip of wood. For the first time, she became aware of the purse clutched in her hand. She scarcely recalled snatching it from where, earlier, she'd tossed it onto the bed. With no time to ponder this apparent reflex and its unexplainable phenomenon of female priorities, she slipped its strap across her shoulder. Both hands free now, she clung to the edge of the window sill and lowered her other foot onto the second bit of doubtful footing. Dismayed to discover there was barely room enough for the ends her toes, Marla inched her way down the wall, clutching the splintery slabs of wood with the tips of her fingers. Inside the cabin, she could hear the angry expletives spewing from the mouth of the intruder. She struggled to control the rasp of her own breathing for fear the sound might reveal her escape route.

Her toes ached, her fingernails were but jagged bits of dorsal covering before she discovered an almost invisible row of narrow cedar projections, positioned alongside the ladder, obviously intended as handgrips. In spite of their limited assistance, Marla began to despair of ever reaching firm ground when two hands closed about her waist, lifting her from the makeshift ladder.

Hands curled into fists, she turned to defend herself, flailing at this interloper who would thwart her escape. "No, no," she gasped. "Leave me alone. Let me go."

"Shhh, don't be afraid." In the darkness she barely made out the features of Jacob Mallory. "You'll be safe now, but we gotta hurry," he urged.

Instinctively, Marla turned toward the pathway leading to the hopeful sanctuary of the Hertz rental car. Instead, his hand firmly grasping her elbow, Jacob guided Marla swiftly across the mesa, toward the bluff where the ship's ladder dangled to the beach below.

She stumbled along beside him, through tangled beach grass snatching at her ankles, while her mind grappled with a tumult of questions. *What was Captain Mallory doing here? Had he been outside, or up in the attic all this time?* She remembered now, the open attic window. There was no time to seek answers. They reached the edge of the mesa. Urging her onto the top rung, her rescuer waited until she had both feet firmly planted on the ladder. Crouching on his knees, he leaned forward until his face was only inches from hers.

"Go, quickly." His command, though whispered, was harsh. "That way." In the dim light Marla could see his arm stretched forward, his finger pointing up the beach, away from the village.

Blindly, she obeyed. In the darkness, the journey down the rock wall was even more harrowing. Only the adrenaline of fear motivated her, kept her fingers clinging to the salt encrusted rope. Her probing foot located the slippery makeshift landing pad, the discarded wooden box placed there earlier. Gratefully, she released her grip upon the ladder and peered upward, expecting to see her rescuer following her down the ladder. But there was no one.

"Jacob?" she hissed into the darkness.

"Go!" The urgent command hurled itself from above.

Hoping she recalled the earlier directive of that outstretched arm, Marla dashed toward the sound of the water, away from the safety of the village. Her legs soon ached as the sand clutched at her feet, like a jealous lover seeking to impede her flight. Pain accompanied each breath she gulped into her tortured lungs. Fear was her running mate; her purse slapping at her side with each step, was like a whip, flogging her on.

Exhaustion finally intervened, halting her journey. Leaning forward, her hands resting upon her knees as she struggled to satisfy the demands of her burning lungs, she listened for sounds of another's breathing. Surely the captain must be close behind. She turned, peering into the darkness for a glimpse of the figure in a foul-weather jacket, the familiar fisherman's cap. Her breath suddenly snagged in her throat, abandoning the plight of her oxygen-starved lungs. Forgotten, too, were tortured, complaining muscles pleading for mercy.

One in being with paralyzing horror, Marla stared at the unnatural brightness hovering above the mesa where, like shooting stars, sparks leaped excitedly into the darkening sky as crackling yellow flames greedily devoured the little gray cabin on the bluff.

An ear-piercing shriek splintered the night air.

Marla felt her body grow numb as the sound sent icy waves of terror washing through her, unaware the screams she heard were her own.

CHAPTER TWENTY-SIX

Shoulders hunched forward, Jacob leaned across the frail form lying upon his father's narrow cot, a station he'd kept during the long, dark hours before dawn. A frown worried his brow as he studied the young woman's pale, fragile features. He'd give anything, he agonized; no, everything, of what little he had left, if he could spare her the trauma she'd suffered this night. He'd tried, God knows, he'd tried every way he knew to discourage her. But she was stubborn, this one, stubborn and persistent, and now, it was too late.

Gently lifting a damp strand of the woman's auburn hair plastering itself across her ashen cheek, he carefully tucked it behind her ear, let his fingers linger a moment on the soft skin at her jaw line. He allowed his thoughts to drift back to the night when, returning from a patrol of the beach in search of firewood, he discovered her curled up on his couch, a book in one hand, an apple in the other, just as though she belonged there. Surprise had been the lesser of his reactions. The loneliness of his self-imposed weeks of exile crowded in upon him. Watching her through the cabin window, a wave of yearning washed over him, and he found himself wishing she did belong there, a wife, a lover, waiting to soothe away the purgatory of a grueling week with the fishing fleet.

Good judgement should have sent him to his father's shanty. Instead, he crawled up the wooden cleats nailed along the cabin wall, and letting himself through thewindow, spent the night in the attic, the mere thought of her presence enough to warm him. He meant her no harm, hadn't meant to frighten her. Still, it was good when she left, putting an end to his fantasy. That should have been, would have been, the end of it, if only she hadn't kept returning to the cabin, stirring up questions in the village with her meddling.

The woman tossed fitfully in her sleep, a frightened whimper slipping past her pale lips. Jacob's strong fingers quickly stilled the agitated fluttering of the hand she lifted from atop the rumpled blankets.

"Shhh, don't fret, Miss Mahla. Everything's gonna be alright."

His whispered reassurance seemed to soothe the demons tormenting her for the young woman lay still again, her lips free, now, from their grimace of fear. A stirring in his loins reminded him of the sensation of those soft lips against his own, the stolen kiss that afternoon he discovered her asleep upon his couch. He knew he was being irrational, indulging an impossible fantasy. If only . . . but, no, there's no place for such thoughts. His father, Sarah, they're both right. In spite of the four short lines in the newspaper, few villagers were aware his boat had burned. It was better for now, safer, to let everyone believe he'd been lost in a storm at sea.

He could still feel the searing heat, the force of the explosion ripping apart the Sea Nymph. Had it not been for an act of fate, he would have been destroyed along with his vessel. Tangled lines prompted him to launch the dinghy to afford better access to troubled nets. Though singed and smarting from his close proximity to the fire, it was from a hard won distance of safety he watched helplessly as the Sea Nymph burned to her water line. The tortuous journey to his father's shanty, the disturbing suspicions that followed, still remained a painful memory.

Had it been an accident? Who knew he'd be taking the boat out alone that day . . . except, maybe his deck hand? Was it merely coincidence Victor failed to show up at the dock that morning? There'd been trouble lately, trouble within the fleet . . . rumors. They decided, he and his father, it would be best for Jacob to remain out of sight for awhile. They needed time to confirm their suspicions; time they lost when this young woman decided to snoop into the affairs of a "phantom seaman."

Jacob gently rubbed his thumb across the welted bruises on Marla's palm where abrasive hemp of the rope ladder had cut cruelly into her flesh. He'd never have believed she'd have the strength, or the courage, to climb the ship's ladder, and more than once at that. His hand tightened tenderly about her bruised one. He had to admit she had a lot of spunk, this lady, spunk and determination. Once she set out to do something, like a bulldog with a bone, she never let go. He liked that about her. If the truth were known, there was a lot about her he liked.

A smile hovered at the corners of his lips. They'd not gone unnoticed either, those unguarded moments when tenderness, creeping into those hazel-green eyes of hers betrayed the young lady's own capricious emotions. The pleasant warmth spreading inside Jacob's chest suddenly turned cold. How would she feel about him, he wondered, once she learned the truth? What would happen when she discovered who set fire to the cabin . . . and why?

CHAPTER TWENTY-SEVEN

The rough-hewn wood of the ceiling wavered in the flickering light of an oil lantern. Marla tried to focus upon the dark stained surface above her, her eyes probing its cracks and crevasses in search of a clue to her surroundings. Slowly, vague recollections stirred in her subconscious. Like movie trailers of coming attractions, startling scenes flashed across her mind. Her body, shivering in the cold night air, strong arms supporting her as she staggered through wet, cloying sand, the vague familiarity of a little room where gentle hands pressed hot liquids past her lips before she was lowered into a cocoon of warm blankets.

Vivid memories elbowed their way to the surface as the obscure took definition. Her frantic gaze darted about the room to where the aspiring light of early morning assaulted the discolored panes of the tiny window above a linoleum-covered counter. Sudden recognition snatched away any lingering remnants of sleep, jolting her upright upon the cot where she had slept away the terrors of the night.

Jeremiah's shanty! She was in Jeremiah's shanty!

The gentle hands so carefully tending to her the night before? Her sluggish memory sought to replay an image of a face hovering over her. Her confused, myopic inspection of her surroundings, stumbling along the cracked and peeling countertop, skittered to a stop. Within her breast, her heart fluttered like a startled bird. A woman stood before a chipped, enamel bowl, her hands immersed in its sudsy water. Although her back was turned, there was no doubt as to her identity, the rigid posture, the wispy knot of gray hair gathered at the nape of her neck, the worn, putrid green cardigan draped about her shoulders. Even before she turned, Marla knew she would be staring into the stern features of the museum's curator.

Mesmerized, Marla watched as the woman dried her hands upon the apron fastened about her waist; remained speechless as, her face twisted into a scowl, the curator approached the cot.

"Well, I hope you're finally satisfied." Arms akimbo, the old woman glared down at Marla. "You never listened to what folks was trying to tell you, did you? Well, now you've gone and made a lot of trouble for yourself and everybody else."

Marla was not prepared for the fierceness of this confrontation, the condemnation she saw in those glittering eyes. "I . . . I don't understand," she stammered. "What am I doing here? How did I get here? What . . .?"

"You're lucky Jacob was looking out for you. You almost got yourself killed!"

"Jacob?" The frightened bird that was her heart trembled in its nest. "Is he . . .?

The woman's jaw tightened, her words forced their way through tight lips. "He's safe, for the time being, anyways. No thanks to you."

"I don't understand. Is Jacob in some sort of danger? What is going on? Please, you must tell me."

There was a barely perceptible softening at the rigid corners of the curator's mouth, a slight relaxing of her stiffened shoulders. Marla could almost hear the grinding wheels of indecisiveness before, averting her eyes the old woman finally spoke.

"It wasn't no accident, what happened to the Sea Nymph." She hesitated, unconsciously tucking a stray strand of graying hair into the its bun. Marla began to despair whether the aged curator was going to continue. When she did, there was a sharpness edging her voice. "It was best for Jacob to let folks think he was lost at sea." The anger returned to the gaze turned back upon Marla. "Until you came along, asking questions, pokin' your nose in where it don't belong."

At that moment, Marla envied the defenseless snail with the haven of its protective shell. She was spared the discomfort of further tongue-lashing when the door to the shanty burst open, diverting the attention of Marla's self-appointed prosecutor. Two figures suddenly shared the small space of the room, both were male, both bundled in foul weather jackets, both wore fishermen's caps. One of them was Jacob Mallory.

Marla had no time to react before he was across the room. Snatching his cap from his head, the young captain dropped to one knee beside the cot where she cowered amidst the tangle of a thin gray blanket.

"You okay, Miss Mahla?"

The small twinge of gratification for this, until now, absent bit of interest in her wellbeing, passed quickly. Marla looked into eyes darkened with concern and struggled to resurrect her power of speech. "Yes . . . yes, I'm fine," she croaked, startled by the strange, rasping sound emitting from her lips. She attempted to clear her throat, but the same harsh, frog-like rasp repeated itself. "Thank you."

Then, unexpectedly, overwhelming remorse for the insensitivity of her curiosity crowded into her chest. "I am so sorry if I've caused you trouble," she whispered.

Relief released the tension of anxiety gripping the fisherman's features, and he shook his head. Dark curls bounced with the motion of his denial. "You don't owe me an apology. I'm just glad you're okay."

"That might not last for long." Marla glanced over Jacob's shoulder to where his father, that rugged Spencer-Tracy-look-alike, scowled down at her. Obviously, he did not share his son's compassion for Marla's circumstance. Beyond his old-man-of the-sea hulk, clattering pans reminded Marla of another's good graces in which she did not reside. Her recent seizure of remorse quickly dissipated. Unspoken questions tumbled about in her mind as her shameless curiosity tugged restlessly at the unfamiliar constraints of exile. Why was Jacob hiding behind the ruse of his supposed death, it demanded? Just how was Jeremiah involved in this ploy? The curator, what put her there at Jeremiah's shanty? And Adonis . . . Marla's mind stumbled as a disturbing image lurked just beyond her recollection. A chill shivered across her shoulders. What was it about the Olympian-like seaman eluding her?

"Maybe you orter to stay out of sight, for awhile, anyways." The old fisherman's speculation snatched Marla back to the present. "Course, as I see it, you don't have a lot of choices no more." Startled, she realized Jeremiah's suggestion was directed, not toward his son, but at her.

Her reaction erupted as temporarily forgotten responsibilities wrested themselves from captivity: the rental car, parked below the cabin, her luggage, her clothing occupying the bedroom closet.

"What do you mean, 'stay out of sight'?" Anxiety sharpened her response. "What about my car, my belongings?"

Three startled gazes turned toward her then were as quickly averted. Then, in that moment, total recollection, like a vengeful tsunami, crushed the fragile cocoon of Marla's self-imposed amnesia. Her clotted memory once again displayed carnivorous flames climbing into the night sky, dancing wildly at the edge of the bluff as they fed hungrily upon the sun-dried shingles of the little gray cabin. Except for one, ragged convulsive gasp ripping itself from somewhere deep inside Marla, silence was master of the small room.

It was Jacob's voice invading the heavy blanket of stillness. Raising his eyes to meet hers, he reached out and gently took her hand in his, its callused roughness that of a man who'd spent a lifetime tending sail lines, hauling fishnets. His voice was as gentle as his hand was hard.

"There're things going on, Miss Mahla, things it's best you not be knowing about." He hesitated, his gaze dropping to where his hand held hers. When he looked up, his eyes were dark with a concern she'd seen there before. "Trouble is, same ones figuring I'm dead, just might be thinkin' you know more than . . .." He hesitated.

"I don't understand." Marla's voice quavered. "What do they think I know? Why would anyone think I know anything about whatever is going on?"

"I'd be afraid they might just start keeping track of you, wantin to know everything you do, everyplace you go."

For some reason, the uneasy memory of her beach walk of several days before crawled across Marla's mind and the "shadow" that followed her as far as the village.

Jacob's fingers, tightening on hers, coincided with a tightening in her chest.

"I don't want anything happening to you, Miss Mahla."

Whether delayed reflex or a reaction to his kindness, Marla felt salty moisture sting her eyelids, then flee in hot rivulets down her cheeks. In an instant, Jacob's arms were around her, pulling her into the rough wool covering his shoulder. Welcoming its abrasive abuse, Marla pressed her face against its harshness, inhaled the musky male odor of its occupant, and gratefully emptied the well of her pent up emotions.

CHAPTER TWENTY-EIGHT

It'd been hours since her companions left: Sarah, the museum's aged curator, presumably returning to her duties at the museum, Jacob and his father headed toward some undisclosed destination. Marla was left alone in the shanty where, as time passed slowly, the confines of the small room became claustrophobic. Despite the dire warnings for her safety, she knew she must escape to the solace of the beach if she was to sort through the confusion of this day's revelations.

Her entire wardrobe now consisting of the tee shirt and jeans she'd been wearing the evening before, she looked about the room for some garment to provide added warmth against the sea air. Her purse dangled from a hook near the door. Beside it hung a well-worn wool shirt, its proportions obviously intended for one of larger dimensions than she. Removing it from its hook, she wriggled her arms into the oversized garment. Retrieving her cell phone from her purse, her only remaining worldly possession, she slipped it into the pocket of her jeans and stepped out into the afternoon sun.

The pungent ocean breeze was like a balm to her blistered nerves, the constancy of the waves, tirelessly kneading the beach, a reassurance of normalcy. Thus placated, she allowed her thoughts to replay the morning's strange scenario with its unexpected surprises, the least not being finding the museum curator tidying Jeremiah's tiny kitchen. Marla had not yet determined the woman's role in this fiasco. Obviously a collaborator in the ruse of Jacob's death, the extent of her association with Jeremiah remained a question. Their conversation that first day at the museum came to mind: Sarah's reference to her earlier association with the deceased Captain Johnson of the *Marcie Dee*. Marla was beginning to suspect it was no shrinking violet sheltered beneath that ugly green cardigan.

Nibbling at the edge of the excitement of Jacob's presence, the assurance of his safety, was the mystery surrounding the choreography of his falsified death. Even more disturbing, and the thought sent a cold chill through Marla, was his allusion to the precariousness of her own position. With a twinge of regret, she once again recalled Naomi's words of caution, words she'd chosen to ignore.

As if on cue, the phone she'd tucked into her pocket startled her with its sudden vibration. Eagerly, she removed it from her pocket and flipped open its cover. It took but a moment to recognize the identity of the caller as Namoi's number appeared on the small screen. Instinctively, Marla moved her finger to the button meant to activate reception, then hesitated. Whatever would she say to her, she wondered; that she'd nearly gotten herself killed last night, that she was hiding out with an old fisherman, an ancient museum curator and a supposedly dead seaman? That would certainly remove any doubts about her sanity. She snapped the lid shut. It would be better to find the answers to her dilemma before talking to anyone.

Tucking the phone into her pocket Marla turned back toward the shanty. She didn't know, just yet, how she'd find those answers but one thing she did know, she had no intention of staying cooped up like some frightened fugitive.

❧　　　❧　　　❧

The two men sat hunched over the small table, their hands wrapped around the warmth of steaming cups of coffee. They glanced up as Marla stepped through the door, the low, masculine sound of their conversation interrupted by her entry. The chastisement Marla read in Jeremiah's eyes generated no guilt; it was the relief in Jacob's eyes that nearly undermined her resolution.

Aware she was the object of their scrutiny, she unhurriedly poured herself coffee from the pot steaming atop the stove, then moved toward the only other available seating, the cot, and settled onto its somewhat lumpy surface. Only then did she raise her eyes to meet theirs.

"Since I seem to be involved in a mess of some sort," she began with a calm she did not feel. "I think it only fair you let me know just what is going on."

The two men glanced uneasily at one another, but it was Jacob who spoke. "You're right, Miss Mahla, there are things you've got a right to know." He turned toward her then, elbows resting on his knees, coffee mug cupped in his hands. Her attention held hostage by the dark seriousness of his gaze, Marla listened as he spoke, his voice, low now, guarded.

"There's some things going on in the fishing fleet, things that . . .well, anybody findin' out has got himself more trouble than a scuppered gillnetter caught in a nor'easter."

He lifted his cup to his lips; Marla watched the muscles contract as the hot liquid traveled down his throat. This was the second time he'd referred to trouble within the fishing fleet. Eyes averted from hers, Jacob stared into the contents of the ceramic mug.

"Things are happening that, for awhile, make it better folks just think I been lost at sea."

"Since you been pokin' around, now they ain't sure." Jeremiah"s interruption was harsh.

Jacob allowed his father's outburst before continuing. "If they figure you know what I know, those who wanted me out of the way might be wantin' to make trouble for you."

The gentle rhythm of Marla's startled heart was interrupted by the sudden emotion she saw in eyes lifted to hers, heard in Jacob's fervent whisper.

"I don't mean to let that happen."

CHAPTER TWENTY-NINE

Marla struggled to match the stride of the tall figure beside her, her frustrated efforts carving invasive gouges in the pristine smoothness of the wet sand. Her fingers clutched futilely at flapping yardage as a persistent wind sought to share the voluminous interior of the oversized woolen shirt she'd confiscated earlier. She was aware of her companion's irritation, which, she seethed inwardly, was certainly no more justified than her own.

"We need to find her a place to stay for three four days" had been Jacob's earlier observation to his father. "Someplace they won't be thinkin' to find her."

"She can't be stayin' here." Jeremiah continued their objective conversation across the top of Marla's head. "'Sides the fact there ain't enough room, it's one of the first places they'd be lookin'."

" I could take her out to the Point. It'd buy us time till we can figure out somethin' else."

"Why can't I just go back to Ed's cabin?" Marla intruded upon this exclusive discussion of her future. "At least there I can make contact with my friends."

A scowl tightened the muscles of Jacob's face. "It's not safe there, either." Annoyance sharpened his retort before mutating itself into a frown of consternation. Then, after a moment's hesitation, "It'd be best if you don't call your friends," Jacob cautioned. "Not for awhile, anyway."

Marla stared in disbelief at the silent but undeniable command in his eyes, then down at his outstretched palm. Surely he didn't expect her to surrender her cell phone, deprive herself of her only contact with the outside world.

"Excuse me?" she countered, certain the derisive tone of her voice clearly conveyed her reaction to his audacious assumption. "You can't be serious."

Her display of defiance did little to alter his intent. His jaw remained firm, his hand thrust forward.

"I suppose if I don't hand it over to you, you'll just sneak into my room and take it."

"It was my father who took your phone," Jacob countered. "That was so you'd not be telling anyone what was going on around here before we were ready. I was the one who took the battery." A scowl crawled across his face. "Seems like that didn't make a difference, though."

To Marla's chagrin, held hostage by that unwavering gaze, she found herself intimidated by its unyielding demand. Ignoring the cautioning nudges of uneasy premonition, she reluctantly tugged the cell phone from her jeans pocket, grudgingly surrendering it into Jacob's waiting palm, her own face twisted into a scowl of displeasure.

Now, floundering alongside this stranger to whom she'd irrevocably relinquished her independence, she was regretting the stupidity of her moment of weakness. Whatever possessed her to put herself at the mercy of his discretion, her destiny in the hands of a man who would willingly promote the fallacy of his death? She glanced toward her companion, his stony features unreadable as, cap pulled low over his forehead, hands shoved into the pockets of his jacket, he leaned into the challenging force of the wind. He chose not to share the knowledge of their destination, identifying it only as "The Point", supposedly a temporary place of safety for Marla. She'd been left little choice but to swallow questions clamoring for satisfaction and meekly follow her dubious benefactor. Submission, so foreign to her independent nature, rankled like a bitter aftertaste upon her tongue.

The encroaching tide had reclaimed the wide expanse of beach, leaving only a narrow avenue of sand available to them. Their journey brought them into a small cove. It was not until she became aware of the bluff towering above them Marla suddenly realized where they were. Purposely, she kept her eyes averted, denying them a temptation to climb the sheer rock wall. She had no desire to view the charred remains of the little gray cabin, responsible for her present predicament. The battered dinghy once languishing at the base of the bluff now rested at the edge of the beach, explaining the earlier whereabouts of Jacob and his father. Water lapped at its stern as Jacob urged the small boat toward the incoming waves.

Not totally convinced of it's degree of safety, Marla balked at the thought of boarding that questionable conveyance, but a glance at the seaman at its stern confirmed she was being offered no option. Obediently, if unwillingly, she stepped across the gunnel and positioned herself upon the seat's damp wood. Slipping into the welcoming arms of the advancing tide, the skiff was soon bobbing upon the surface of the bay. Oars, having been retrieved from their undisclosed hiding place and stationed in their oarlocks, squeaked and groaned as Jacob pulled against the tide's gravitational flow. The small craft shot forward with each thrust of the glistening blades.

From where she sat facing her captain, Marla could study the features of Jacob Mallory at leisure. They differed little from the face in the museum photo, she concluded, stronger perhaps, but with the same somber melancholy overtones. The shadowy depths of the dark eyes remained unreadable. The captain had loosened the buttons of his jacket to accommodate the physical labors of rowing, displaying the flex of hardened muscles as they strained against the woolen shirt stretched across the broad expanse of his chest. Perhaps it was this unguarded moment of familiarity encouraging Marla to renew the subject of their proposed destination.

"Look, I don't know where this "Point" you speak of is," she argued, " but I see no reason why I can't just stay at Ed's cottage. Besides, I need to contact my friends, I know they'll be worried about me."

There was no response from her self-appointed protector, but the stern set of his jaw suggested any future efforts at conversation were destined for failure. She was left with no choice but to surrender her attention to the hypnotic monotony of the flat tipped oars, each rhythmic dip and rise flinging a copious spray of water her way as they sliced across the surface of the bay.

By what degree of back stiffness or derriere numbness she fretted, did one determine nautical distance? She'd lost track of time, had no idea how much longer she was expected to endure the discomfort of this lurching, bucking derelict. Judging from the misery of her body, jarred into a bundle of aching muscles by each jolt of the bouncing skiff, the seemingly unending journey was to be eternal. A capricious wind, forerunner of an impending storm, agitated the water of the bay, teasing it into angry waves.

Further aggravating Marla's irritability was the steady, unbroken rhythmic movements of her oarsman. Seemingly undisturbed by the altered weather conditions, he continued to doggedly pull at the oars, the methodical squeaking of their oarlocks a testimony to his stubborn determination. Misty fog all but obliterated sight of the distant shoreline, the only scrap of security during this torturous, joyless pilgrimage. The shirt she'd confiscated for warmth was no longer fulfilling its intended purpose. Salty sea spray had molded her hair into a stiff, unflattering coif while the brackish residue encrusted her lips. Marla tentatively ran her tongue over their saline coating, then, never one to suffer in silence, opened her mouth to protest.

"Captain Mallory?" A dry croak escaped her well of misery. " How much longer . . .? "

Her intended plea for mercy was cut short by the abrasive sound of sand scraping along the hull of the boat. In the same instant, Jacob abandoned the oars, leaping from the bow onto a sandy spit where the craft now rested. Marla was impressed by the ease with which, grabbing the bow with both hands, he effortlessly dragged the unwieldy vessel higher onto the gritty shore. Eager to be free from the abuse of this sea going torture chamber, she gratefully accepted his proffered helping hand. To her distress, she discovered her legs, cramped too long in one position, chose not to respond to her attempt to scale the gunnel. Dismay became embarrassment when, in the next instant, Marla felt herself being scooped into strong arms and lifted across what a moment before seemed an insurmountable obstacle.

Her line of vision now directed over Jacob's shoulder, she noticed through a misty shroud of fog, the tall, cone-shaped structure towering above them. Sudden realization came with recognition. Jacob had delivered her to the lighthouse on that tip of land jutting out into the far end of the bay, a tip of land apparently known as "The Point."

CHAPTER THIRTY

It was small but cozy, the room assigned as hers. A narrow bed occupied one wall, while against the opposite panel of knotty pine, a tiny table and chair served as both desk and dining space. Tucked into one corner, a potbellied stove challenged any chill that might slip past the thick, insulated walls. Its only other door besides the entry, Jacob informed her, provided access to both the main kitchen and bathroom facilities.

Marla resigned herself to the moment, helpless to do little else. With the reassurance of a quick return, Jacob left to make their arrival known to the lighthouse keeper, who, it appeared, was occupant of the quarters at the other end of this light keeper's cottage, and Marla's only source of companionship for the next few days.

Only minutes passed before her self-appointed guardian once again stood at her side.

"You'll be safe here," Jacob assured her. "If you need anything, let Zeb know, he'll look after you 'til I get back."

"What I need is to know what is going on."

With an infuriating shrug of dismissal, her companion, ignoring her persistent demand, turned his attention t o the pot bellied stove.

"Seems a mite cold in here. I better start you a fire before I go."

Kneeling before the room's sole source of heat, the captain unlatched its grated door. With fraying patience, Marla watched as Jacob's strong, tanned hands transferred dry driftwood from the wood box into the stove's iron belly until her exasperation could no longer be suppressed.

"Why won't you tell me?" she persevered. "Why have you brought me here to this God-forsaken place? I've a right to know."

Angry words, waiting their turn at her lips, crawled back into her throat as Jacob rose to face her. A shadow of melancholy clouded his features, veiling the darkness of his eyes.

"I'm sorry, Miss Mahla. It's just best for you not to be knowin'."

Marla felt the warmth of Jacob's broad hands on her shoulders and for a moment, thought he might embrace her, even found herself wishing he would. But instead, he dropped his hands to his sides.

"You're just gonna have to trust me."

Marla watched in silence as Jacob turned and walked away, closing the door behind him. A simmering rebellion temporarily subdued by the trauma of a harrowing sea journey, suddenly erupted, spewing forth the lava of her anger. *Surrender my destiny to the whim of a couple of chauvinistic fishermen? I don't think so, not until I've untangled the cat's cradle woven about this elusive sea captain.*

Yet, despite her self-righteous defiance, a small dissident voice inside whispered, "Oh, yes, Jacob. I trust you. I do trust you."

❦   ❦   ❦

Marla spent the next half-hour visually re-examining the confines of her faux prison where, from all indications, she would be expected to reside for an indefinite period of time. A victim of claustrophobia, she might have been disturbed by the prospect of such restrictive confinement had the large west window not promised a beautiful view of Cape Cod sunsets across the bay. However, it seemed she'd have to forego that pleasure for awhile. The only view afforded her now was the fearsome approach of a New England storm, its churlish winds churning the waters; its glowering clouds darkening the sky.

A sudden, searing illumination of lightening filled the room. A rumbling explosion shuddered overhead, and an instant later the westerly window with its promise of sunset views was awash with a watery onslaught flung from the shattered black clouds above.

Marla stared into the magnificent display of nature's force, but her only thoughts were of Jacob. *Did he make it safely back to Jeremiah's ahead of the storm?*

CHAPTER THIRTY ONE

In the two days following Jacob's departure into an approaching storm, Zeb, a wiry seaman in his long-of-tooth years, proved to be all the captain promised. While not a vocal companion, he was attentive to Marla's needs, delivering a tasty, if sparse, meal to her quarters each night. As if sensing her concern, he volunteered assurance of Jacob's safe arrival at his father's shanty. Although not certain how he knew, not having seen evidence of a telephone, Marla eagerly welcomed the comfort of his offering.

However, as each long, boring day passed, she became more and more restless, impatient with the uncertainty of her future. In spite of her persistent questioning, Zeb offered little enlightenment, leaving no doubt in her mind, he, too, shared in this collusion involving the captain of the Sea Nymph.

At first, exploring the lighthouse, to which she'd been given total access, helped fill the vacuum of time. The view was spectacular, worth the challenge of the thirty-eight-step climb to the tower. From its lofty vantage she was rewarded with, not only the westerly panorama of the bay, but to the north and east, a view of the endless expanse of the Atlantic Ocean. To the south, beyond the jumble of rip-rap surrounding the lighthouse, a small rutted road provided the only land access across the isolated stretch of land separating them from civilization. From her observation post, the nearest so-called civilization appeared to be a small, disorderly cluster of buildings, assumedly another fishing village, made barely discernable by distance.

It wasn't long before Marla depleted all available options for combating the empty void of inactivity. She read brochures, scanned nautical maps, studied regularity of the tides, even ingesting never-to-be-used information regarding how high and low air pressures controlled the weather. In spite of its "dinosauric" allure, the only visitation to the lighthouse apparently the sporadic arrival of a truck delivering mail and supplies. Marla covetously contemplated the next arrival of this vehicle as perhaps a means of escape from her unwelcome captivity. Meanwhile, as of yet, she'd not witnessed the actual occurrence of this clandestine event.

Today, Marla lingered in her morning shower letting its lethargic stream of tepid water coax her body from sleep, while she considered the questionable merit of hiking out of this desolation. That alternate, if not practical, plan gathered appeal as she reluctantly pulled on the tired jeans and tee shirt she'd worn for the last three days. The improbability of such an undertaking faded before the giddy prospect of a clean change of clothing. Somehow, without arousing suspicion, she needed to determine the distance to that little fishing village and, hopefully, contact with the outside world.

Completing her morning toiletries, Marla wandered toward the lighthouse, mentally outlining her forthcoming confrontation with that stoic keeper of the light. Zeb was nowhere in sight. She stepped into the foyer of the lighthouse, thinking perhaps to find the object of her search at work in his tower.

"Zeb?" Her voice climbed the spiral stairway, echoing hollowly off the walls of the concrete tube. "Hello?"

Although she'd raised her voice a decibel higher, there still was no answer. Zeb appeared to be occupied elsewhere. She was about to step back into the misty morning when a small table stationed beneath the stair well captured her attention. A disorderly sprawl of envelopes and periodicals covered its surface. A disturbing realization agitated the breakfast she'd consumed just a short time before. The mail truck had arrived . . . and departed while she slept.

Disappointment exonerated her from any feelings of guilt as she leafed dejectedly through the uninteresting collection of political circulars, advertisements and sundry nautical publications. The only item challenging the lethargy of her interest was a very thin edition of a local newspaper. Listlessly, she released its folds to where a front page headline announced the impending exposure of a suspected crab poaching operation involving local fishermen. Idly, she let her disinterested gaze slide down the page, skimming through the scandalous details of illegal harvesting of the area's endangered blue crab. Violations included night poaching, disregard of size restrictions and trafficking in the black market.

It was not the account's chilling inference of a suspected arson suddenly capturing Marla's attention, snatching the breath from her lungs. Leaping from the printed surface, bold letters identified a small, two inch article tucked at the bottom of the page: *Missing Woman Feared Dead.*

Heart crowding into the back of her throat, Marla quickly scanned the few lines that followed. *Two Seattle airline employees, vacationing on the Cape, have reported the disappearance of a third member of their party. An investigation by Boston authorities led to the discovery of the woman's rental car parked outside a cabin recently destroyed by fire. Although no body has been found, it is feared the woman may have perished in the blaze. No further details are available at this time.*

Oh, lordy! The newsprint in her hands blurred as Marla felt the blood drain from her face, her knees threaten to give way beneath her. *Perished in the fire? Lordy, lordy! Reba and Naomi must think I'm dead!* She had to get to a phone!

The discarded tattle-tell pages slithered from her inert fingers, scattering to the floor behind her as she leaped down the steps of the lighthouse and across its concrete apron. She gave no thought to her destination, only the need to find Zeb and a phone to the outside world. Her frantic gaze searched the barren outpost, probed the space surrounding the cottage then swung to where the waters of the bay incessantly massaged the sandy beach.

There she saw him, his tall, lanky frame bent forward in a posture of haste, the unmistakable figure of Captain Mallory. She shortened the distance between them with hurried steps of her own. It did not occur to her to question the timing of his arrival; she was only aware of an overwhelming relief he was there.

"Jacob!" Her fingers clutched frantically at the lapels of his jacket. "I've got to call them, Jacob!" Marla fought to control an aching lump of hysterical sobs bubbling in her chest. "They think I'm dead!"

As Jacob's hands closed tightly over hers, Marla struggled to regain her self-command, to absorb strength from the firmness of his grip. Still, she could not control the tremor creeping into her voice.

"Why would they do that, Jacob?" she babbled. "Why would they print such a story?"

Only vaguely aware of the arm encircling her waist, of being guided away from the beach, Marla renewed her incoherent pleas "What's going on, Jacob? What's happening?"

Not until Jacob opened the door, gently encouraged her across the threshold did Marla realize he'd delivered her to her quarters at the lighthouse.

Seating her at the room's one small table, the sea captain lowered himself into the chair opposite hers. For the first time, she noticed the folded newspaper protruding from the pocket of his jacket. Tugging it from its enclosure, he placed it on the table between them. Somehow, Marla knew even without seeing the headlines, it was a copy of the same periodical she'd left lying on the lighthouse floor.

Leaning across the table, Jacob imprisoned Marla's frantic gaze with the intensity of his own dark one. "Miss Mahla, there're bad things happening in the village." His voice was soft, scarcely above a whisper. "There's trouble I'm wishin' you hadn't come into. But it's too late for wantin' things different." He reached toward the newspaper.

Marla shook her head. "I've read it."

A dark eyebrow lifted in momentary surprise. Capturing her hands in his, the captain continued. "Then, you mostly know what's been going on. What you don't know is . . .." His fingers tightened on hers. She heard the sound of air being drawn into his lungs. " Miss Mahla, the cabin was set ablaze on purpose. It was meant you should die in that fire."

Marla snatched her hand from its haven of comfort; the struggle for air now being hers as shock ricocheted through her body. "But why?" she gasped. "Why?"

Her mind disabled by shock, Marla did not resist as Jacob reclaimed the cold clamminess of her hands, capturing them once again in his own. Vaguely aware of despair at their departure, she welcomed the warmth of their return.

"When Victor showed up at the cabin that night, I figured he was somehow mixed up with the troubles in the fishing fleet." Jacob explained carefully. "I knew then he was up to no good. I just didn't know how desperate he was."

"Victor?" Marla's mind replayed the image of Adonis's muscular frame, looming in the cabin doorway.

"Victor was my deck hand. I figure now, he was the one who set fire to my boat."

"Why would he set fire to your boat?" Marla's mind groped for some meaning in Jacob's words.

"I'd been suspecting for awhile the Sea Nymph was being run nights after I'd moored her at the dock. Then, there was talk around about illegal crab harvesting going on in the Bay . . . pilfering of crab traps." He spoke slowly as if wanting to give Marla time to digest his explanation. "I got to thinking maybe the Nymph was being used in that poaching." After a slight hesitation, Jacob continued. "Somebody who didn't take kindly to my nosing around figured the way to get rid of me and the evidence was to set the boat afire." The captain paused, his jaw tightening with unwelcome recollection. "It appears now that somebody was Victor."

"But why do you let everyone think you're dead?"

"I have to prove it wasn't an accident, the burning of the Sea Nymph. I need time to clear her name, find out who destroyed her. Nearly everybody thinkin' I'm dead gives me that time."

"It doesn't make sense, why would he -- Victor-- burn your cabin, why would he want me dead?"

Releasing her hands, Jacob clenched his own into fists of frustration on the table in front of him. Marla could read impatience in his expression.

"Miss Mahla, you've got to understand!" There was a harsh edge to his voice now. "Poachers ain't gonna stand by if they figure you're meddling in their affairs. You being dead would get rid of any chance of them being found out. Letting them think you died in that fire, well, it'll keep you safe and give me more time for what I gotta be doing."

He tore his angry gaze from her startled one, stared down at his hands, no longer curled into fists, resting on the table in front of him. Several moments passed before he spoke, his voice reflecting a heart-stopping gentleness Marla witnessed in the eyes he raised to meet hers.

" I know you' re frettin', Miss Mahla, about your friends thinking you bein' dead." Tugging an object from his pocket, he placed it upon the table. "So I won't stop you from calling them. But if you could wait awhile, just give me a little more time . . .."

Marla stared at the cell phone lying between them, her longed for connection to the outside world, her liberation. It was possible, now, for her to call Naomi and Reba, return to Seattle, her structured life, her job at the travel agency, her comfortable uptown apartment and its closet full of fashionable "size ten" clothing. Or, she could choose to remain here, here in the nebulous world of Jacob Mallory, supposedly deceased captain of the now defunct Sea Nymph.

She raised her eyes to meet the questioning gaze across from her, stared into its dark, seemingly fathomless depths. She hesitated for only an instant, then, with trembling fingers, reached for her cell phone.

CHAPTER THIRTY-TWO

Closing her fingers around the cell phone, Marla lifted it from the table's smooth surface, then quickly dropped the small black box into the pocket of the oversized shirt, now a permanent part of her wardrobe.

Never would she have anticipated the reward she received, the breathtaking smile transforming the face of the man seated across from her. Later, she would describe it to Reba as "a smile to die for" but at the moment, her heart stumbled, then merely fluttered weakly amid a delirium of pleasure at his beamed approval.

" First off," her companion unfolded the newspaper resting at his elbow and jabbed a finger at the startling headline. "You read this so you know what I gotta do."

Marla forced her attention to the oversized letters splashing their message across the page and tried to understand how this revelation of illegal operations affected the captain. "I guess I didn't read it all," she confessed. "After I saw the article about myself, I just . . ."

"This part, right here." His jabbing finger impatiently directed Marla's attention to the lower section of the article from where, earlier, it had been so shockingly diverted. "Here, where it talks about my boat bein' burned, about it maybe bein' arson. Once they find out I ain't dead, that the Sea Nymph was bein' used for poaching, they sure as fire are gonna figure I burned my own boat as a cover up."

An unexpected chill of foreboding dissolved Marla's lingering state of euphoria. "What could they do?" she countered. "If they launch an investigation; find out you weren't killed in the fire . . .?" Panic accompanied a sudden awareness of the dangers facing the man seated across from her. "What if the poachers try to kill you again?" Frightened words leapt from her lips, "Oh, lordy, you can't stay here in Cape Cod. You can't risk being discovered."

"What I plan to do is find Victor." Jacob interrupted. "I figure him bein' the one guilty of arson, he's knowing who else is mixed up in the poaching."

"But what if he refuses to admit to it?" Marla agonized.

"I don't figure that to be a problem." The grim set had returned to Jacob's jaw. "The problem will be in finding him. I can't be lettin' myself seen around the marina, but, I figure that's where he hangs out, sleeping on boats moored there for the night, like maybe he was doing on the Sea Nymph."

A sudden image flashed across Marla's mind; smudged windows, indistinct but undeniably the face of Adonis peering from behind them. "Wait," she gasped. "Jacob, I think I know where he is." Her words tumbled over one another in the excitement of her recollection. "I saw him at Mrs. Doolittle's boarding house, when I was looking for a place to rent. I'm sure that's where he's staying."

Her heart tripped as the smile, though perhaps not as sensuous as before, returned to Jacob's lips.

❦   ❦   ❦

"Absolutely not! I refuse to stay here another day!" Marla couldn't believe Jacob would suggest such a thing, not after she'd so accommodatingly given him a clue to the whereabouts of Adonis. . . or Victor . . ., or whoever he was. "I'm going back with you."

"That makes no sense." There was a chauvinistic sternness in Jacob's retort. " I know this ain't easy for you, but there's no place else safe as here."

The hint of compassion shadowing his words gave Marla courage to pursue her challenge. "I can stay at Ed's cottage. Your father has the key. Nobody else needs to know I'm there."

"People in the village pretty much know everything that goes on in the Cape," he argued. "Not much chance of keepin' that kind of secret."

"I'll stay out of sight, I promise. Please, Jacob," she pleaded, donning an unfamiliar but what she hoped was a suitably subservient, obedient, woman-in-distress expression. She didn't experience the pleasure she'd expected at the success of this female ploy as she watched the captain's agitated struggle with indecision.

"I 'spose we can try." With a defeated sigh, he finally, if reluctantly, conceded. "But I'm not likin' it."

At that moment Marla had no idea what Jacob planned to do, in fact, had given little thought to whether he would confront Victor at the boarding house, or direct the authorities to his place of hiding. She was too pre-occupied with elation at having attained her goal ... freedom from her lighthouse prison.

❧   ❧   ❧

Marla snuggled into the comforting arms of Ed's overstuffed easy chair, gazed out across the sand dunes where tufts of beach grass were silhouetted against the fading twilight of the day. She'd been successfully delivered to the dwelling she'd shared with her friends only a few days past, but what now seemed like an eternity ago. In spite of the fact she'd been inundated with adamant restrictions: "stay put inside the cottage, don't be lightin' no fires in the fireplace, don't be burnin' no lamps after dark," she felt secure, safe in familiar surroundings. She could now turn her meandering thoughts back to Jacob and how he intended to use the information she'd given him concerning the whereabouts of Victor.

Warmth, like sweet honey, flowed through her at the thought of Jacob, his concern for her safety, his efforts to spirit her, undetected, from the bleakness of the lighthouse to the haven of Ed's cottage. The return trip across the bay somehow seemed shorter, less harrowing, with Marla knowing the journey would lead to her longed for emancipation. Jeremiah reacted true to form upon learning the cottage was to be the final destination. Given little choice, the wheels of the plan already in motion, he finally surrendered the key, but not without dire predictions of the consequence of their rash actions. Marla's heart fluttered as she remembered the parting concern in Jacob's eyes as he stood in the doorway of the cottage.

"Lock this door when I leave," he ordered sternly. "Don't you be openin' it to nobody but me." To her surprise, he leaned forward and she felt their warmth as his lips brushed against hers; heard the soft whisper of his voice against her cheek.

"You take care, now. I'll be back, soon as I can."

He was gone then, she supposed to return to his father's shanty. For the first time, Marla abandoned her self-indulgent thoughts; turned them toward Jacob and his unvoiced intentions. Did he intend to confront Victor? She wondered what would happen when the two men met face to face. An uncontrollable chill shuddered up her spine.

CHAPTER THIRTY-THREE

Marla despaired over the turn her thoughts had taken, leading her into a sea of anxiety and mental anguish. She resented the helplessness she felt, being deposited out of harm's way like some willful, but ineffectual, child. With no knowledge of what was going on, she was left to chomp at the bit of impatience and frustration. What if something dire should happen to Jacob? What would become of her, then? How long before Jeremiah, or even Ed, for that matter, would think to visit the cottage? Despair became her roommate, uncertainty purloining any hope of a peaceful night of sleep.

An earlier foray through the cupboards produced only the few staples left behind when her last visit was aborted. Denied the option of visiting the local grocer, she disparaged the thought of surviving on a menu of cold cereal, saltine crackers and redundant servings of Dinty Moore stew. Still, she hesitated to defy Jacob's directives.

Even more distressing was the abomination of allowing her friends, Naomi and Reba, to believe she was dead. Loyalty, nurtured by the history of their friendship dictated she call them, at least let them know she was alive. She considered the precaution of asking them not to reveal her whereabouts. Certainly that would avoid any interference with Jacob plans.

Probing into the pocket of the shirt hanging on a hook by the door, Marla retrieved her cell phone. Flipping open its cover she paused, fingers hovering uncertainly above the tiny digits, interrupted by a disturbing afterthought. A discerning Naomi would, without doubt, appear outside the cottage door within hours. She could call Reba, but could the young agent be trusted to keep the information to herself?

Past experience cautioned against the unlikely. And yet, Marla knew she must make contact with her friends. Taking a deep breath, she punched in the code that would connect her with Reba.

Never had a voice sounded so beautiful to Marla. She selfishly delayed the disappointment of its loss, then, "Hi Reba," she announced softly. "It's me, Marla."

There was empty silence and, for a moment, Marla feared their connection had been broken. The following screech, all but perforating her eardrum, convinced Marla otherwise.

"Marla? Marla! You're alive! I knew it! I knew it! I told Naomi! I just knew you were alive! Oh, wait till I call her! You haven't called her have you? I can't wait to see her face! I can't wait to tell her!"

"Reba. Reba, listen to me." Marla quickly shouldered her way into the excited tirade. "That's exactly what you mustn't do. You mustn't tell anyone about this call, not even Naomi. Do you understand, Reba?"

"What do you mean? Of course, I must tell Naomi. She needs to know. What are you saying, Marla? What's happened? Where are you?"

Too late, Marla recognized the call as a mistake. "I'm fine, Reba. Honestly." She groped for an explanation that would placate her friend. "It's just, well, I promised someone I wouldn't say where I am until . . . it's only for a little while. I just didn't want you to worry, Reba."

"This has something to do with that dead sailor, doesn't it? Are you in some kind of trouble, Marla? I think I should come over there. I can take some of my sick leave."

"No, no, don't do that, Reba. Everything is fine, really. Look, I'm staying at Ed's place. I'll call you in a couple of days. Promise me you won't say anything until I call you, okay?"

She listened to a disquieting dead air space between them, and then Reba's voice, subdued, uncertain, crawled from the cell phone. "Okay, Marla. But, be sure to call me . . . in two days. Okay?"

"Or sooner," Marla vowed, already regretting her rash decision. Harboring secrets had never been Reba's forte. She cringed at the thought of the repercussions of the call; the Pandora's box her moment of weak self-indulgence opened.

It was impossible to "unring" the bell so there was little else to do but wait . . . and hope. In an effort to dispel her uneasiness, Marla applied herself to the problems at hand. Wrapping herself in a bed sheet, she tossed the entirety of her existing wardrobe into the steaming waters of the washing machine. For good measure, she added the confiscated oversized shirt. What a blessing it would be to slip back into clean smelling garments again.

❦   ❦   ❦

Marla struggled to escape the cloying remnants of sleep, prying her eyes open to the light filtering through the muslin curtains and filling the room with the brightness of a midday sun. It surprised her she'd slept soundly through the night, considering the tormenting horde of worry-laden gremlins following her into her bed. But now, something reached into her deep slumber, urging her into wakefulness. She strained against the clinging arms of Morpheus; sought to identify what disturbed her rest. She heard it then, the insistent jingle of her cell phone clamoring for attention from atop the bedside table.

Alertness was slow in arriving. Automatically, she reached for the phone, flipped open its cover, and pressing it to her ear, responded to its demand. "Hello?" Too late, warnings of caution activated her brain.

The voice reaching into her ear was a familiar one, one she'd heard only a few hours earlier.

"Hi, Marla. It's me, Reba. Now don't be mad, but I just had to come. Something is wrong, I can tell. I didn't call Naomi, like you asked, but you know she's going to be upset, for sure. Anyway, I managed to get on a red-eye flight to Boston and I'm here at Mo's café now, having a cup coffee. I wanted to call first; make sure you're still at the cottage."

At that moment, Marla was more certain than ever she never should have made the call to her friend. Dear, sweet Reba. She didn't want her mixed up in this mess.

"Yes, Reba, I'm still at Ed's. But, look, Hon, it's better if you don't come here. I . . ."

"I'm on my way over. And oh, by the way, guess who I ran into here at the café? Remember that good looking fisherman . . . ?"

The click interrupting Reba's chatter was followed by ominous dead air space. "Hello? Reba? Reba?"

Terror swept away any remnants of lassitude. *Oh, lordy*, the good looking fisherman, Adonis...Victor, the man who tried to kill her. He was with Reba. He knew by now she was at the cottage, knew she was still alive. Scrambling from the bed sheets, Marla slipped quickly into her freshly washed lingerie, jammed her feet into the legs of her jeans. *Oh, Jacob, where are you? Where are you?*

Marla hesitated, her arm thrust halfway into the sleeve of her tee shirt as a frightening thought slashed across the turbulence of her mind. If Victor was still around, then what about Jacob, what happened to him? Desperation became her persecutor. Whatever should she do? Who could she call for help? Jeremiah? Sarah? She yanked the tee shirt down over her head. Nine one, one! The emergency numbers clawed their way through her anxiety. She could call nine one, one. A fleeting memory of her last encounter with that dispatcher skittered across her mind. *Oh, lordy.* But she had no choice. She had to call somebody and there was nobody she could call . . . nobody but nine one, one.

CHAPTER THIRTY-FOUR

Jamming his hands deeper into the pockets of his foul-weather jacket, Jacob lengthened the angry stride carrying him along the narrow strip of sand. "What the hell was I thinking?" he cursed beneath his breath.

To have come this far, he derided himself; this close to finding the answers he'd been looking for, then caving in; scuttling into port like some wimpy, seasick greenie, at the first threatening gust of a nor'easter. His memory mocked him with the young woman's mask of distress, luring him from his better judgement. An annoyed toss of his head failed to dislodge the unpleasant retrospection.

The lighthouse was the safest place for her, he fumed inwardly. With Zeb to look after her, he'd have been able to center all his attention on tracking Victor, putting names to the guilty poachers who were threatening the very livelihood of the Cape's fishing fleet. Now, he didn't have the time he'd hoped for, time afforded him by Sarah, Jeremiah and the handful of villagers sheltering the secret of his survival. With already one attempt on her life, Jacob knew he must move quickly before Victor discovered his intended victim, the victim he thought had died in the cabin fire, was still alive and hiding in Ed Balcom's cottage.

🍁   🍁   🍁

Avoiding the main street of the village, Jacob worked his way to its outskirts and Mrs. Dolittle's boarding house where Marla claimed to have seen Victor. He wasn't all that enthused about confronting the feisty landlady. She'd never been one of his favorites; wasn't, as far as he knew, one of those villagers made privy to his secret. Could she be trusted, he wondered, with the knowledge he was alive? He shrugged his shoulders. He really didn't see he had much choice.

Once she recovered from the shock of seeing the "presumably-lost-at-sea" fisherman standing on her doorstep, Mrs. Doolittle turned out to be an eager, though less than helpful, collaborator. Victor was not in, she disclosed, had not shown up for several days. But she was more than willing to testify to her boarder's strange, nocturnal activities, the late night comings and goings, the furtive gatherings in his third story bedroom with "some of them fellas he hangs out with down at the Blue Crab."

She didn't tolerate such goings on in her boarding house, the indignant landlady informed Jacob with a defiant lift of her chin. After all, she had certain rules, and those rules were not to be ignored. Jacob left a righteous Mrs Doolittle standing in her doorway, arms akimbo, declaring to all within earshot, the irrefutable merits of her reputable establishment

Jacob made the Blue Crab his next stop, a bawdy, waterfront pub frequented by unmarried and married fishermen alike, and one he knew to be Victor's favorite haunt. Jacob paused outside the squatty, shed-like building, the low-grade blue coat of paint peeling from its weathered boards-and-bats siding. Once he showed his face inside, disproved the theory of his death, Jacob was aware it would only be a matter of hours before the entire village knew of it, including the poachers he hoped to identify. He must decide upon his priorities: his own vindication or the safety of the young woman haunting his every waking hour. He needed no time for second thoughts; his decision was already made. Caution no longer an option; he pushed open the faded blue doors.

The room was nearly empty, it being too early in the day for the gathering of fishermen now tending their nets. Only one beached-by-age sailor hunkered over the counter, staring into his mid-morning pint of ale. From the bartender, astonished at finding himself facing a returned-from-the-dead seaman, Jacob learned Victor had left the establishment but a short time before.

"Took off like a banshee out of Hades, he did," the barkeep supplied having regained his stoic demeanor. "Soon as he heard Spence here had seen one of them airline women up at Mo's. But ain't that Victor for ya?" he added with a wry chuckle. "Allus out trollin' for women."

Apprehension crawled up Jacob's spine on tiny cold feet. The information he'd just received could mean only one thing; if Marla's friends were back, her whereabouts, if it had not already been revealed, would soon be discovered. His time had run out, along with his options. He saw no choice now but to turn himself over to the authorities; solicit their help in apprehending Victor and his cohorts . . . before it was too late.

He was at the police station, being interrogated by government agents investigating recent crab poaching allegations, when the phone call came, a frantic woman, afraid for her life, calling for help.

CHAPTER THIRTY-FIVE

The dreaded interaction with the emergency operator went more easily than Marla anticipated, the operator being patient and sympathetic. Once able to sort through the incoherence of Marla's near hysteria, the dispatcher quickly transferred the call to the police department.

"He's on his way over," Marla blurted into the responding officer's ear "He wants to kill me. Please, somebody . . . ."

"Hold on, lady," the gruff voice interceded. "Slow down. Who's on his way over to where? Who wants to kill you?"

"Adonis, no, no, I mean Victor," Marla babbled. "He tried to kill me once. He thinks I know about his poaching, about him setting fire to Jacob's boat." Like frenzied fish spilling from the restraint of a fisherman's net, her frantic words tumbled over one another. "He's the one who set fire to Jacob's cabin. Jacob will tell you."

"Jacob? You mean Captain Mallory?"

"Yes, yes, Jacob Mallory. He tried to kill him too." Marla wanted to crawl into the phone, grab this man by his shirt collar and shake him into understanding the need for haste.

"Who am I talking to?" There was a sharp edge to the officer's voice.

"Patterson, I'm Marla Patterson. Please, officer . . . ."

His voice muted, the officer spoke to someone away from the phone, then, "Where you at, Miss Patterson?"

"Ed's cottage, Ed Balcolm."

"Just stay where you are, we'll be right there."

"Oh, please, hurry."

Having secured the doors and windows, Marla could only wait; wait and hope the officers' arrival preceded that of Victor's. A disturbing thought surfaced in the quicksand of anxiety engulfing her. What about Reba, would she be with Victor? Why did she hang up so quickly? Uneasily, Marla flipped open her cell phone, once again poked in Reba's code. There was no response. *Why doesn't she answer? What's happened to her? If she's been hurt . . . dear God, this is my fault.* Guilt twisted itself into a knot inside her chest. What disastrous mayhem had she caused with her persistent meddling?

Marla's painful self-recrimination was interrupted by the rattling sound as someone jiggled the doorknob; the dull thud of someone's weight hurtled against the oaken panel. *Victor, it must be Victor! Where are the police? Oh, lordy, what should I do, where can I hide?* Marla's frantic gaze raked the suddenly too small interior of the living room, clawed wildly at the doors leading to the bedrooms. There was no place to hide . . . nowhere he wouldn't find her. She had to escape. Her eyes darted to the patio entry. Beyond its glass panels the wide expanse of the beach beckoned, its sandy dunes promising hopeful, though tenuous, refuge.

Marla slid the glass enclosures aside; flung herself through their opening, not bothering to close them behind her. The sand's cold, granular surface gave way beneath her feet, its gritty grains swallowing her stumbling stride, impeding her desperate flight. Terror fragmented all reasoning when, from the haven she'd just left, Victor's angry expletives hurled themselves after her, his heavy footsteps pounding the damp earth in pursuit. Frantically, Marla struggled against the yielding farina-like particles eagerly engulfing her faltering steps.

Raucous shouts splintered the air. A sudden cacophony of male voices swarmed after her like angry bees. "Stop!" a harsh command. "Stop or I'll shoot!" She dared not stop, dared not surrender to the futility of her efforts. Her breath slashed cruelly at her throat, ripping itself from her lungs in convulsive sobs. Her legs were but extensions of pain: her thighs, her calves, screaming for mercy. She could go no further. Her pursuer was but a few steps away; so close she could hear the labors of his breathing. She felt his hand upon her shoulder. Sobbing helplessly, she turned, flailed weakly at her assailant. He folded strong arms around her, imprisoned her in a vice-like embrace, drawing her trembling body close to his.

"Miss Mahla," he panted into her ear. "It's me, Jacob. It's okay. Everything's okay. You're safe now."

CHAPTER THIRTY-SIX

Back in her own apartment, Marla smiled at the two people seated across from her, two of the dearest people in her life. Naomi and Reba rewarded her with smiles of their own. Marla sighed, sank back into her favorite recliner, luxuriating in the softness of silk lounging pajamas caressing her skin. She'd forgotten how wonderful it could be, surrounded by her own possessions, her closest friends.

Naomi set her wine goblet atop the glass-topped coffee table, her smile replaced by a frown of reproach. "I still haven't forgiven you two," she scolded. "How could you not let me know what was happening, Marla; that you were still alive?"

Marla didn't need to be reminded of her decision to exclude her friend from news of her non-death. "I am sorry, Naomi. It was thoughtless of me. But I didn't want you coming back to the Cape, getting mixed up in that mess." Marla cast her own glance of reproach toward her younger friend. "Of course, I had no idea Reba would do the very thing I was trying to avoid." She quickly softened her reprimand with a smile of gratitude. "Though, now, I'm glad you did, Hon. It may well have saved my life."

"I can't believe our Adonis, or, whatever his name – Victor - turned out to be such an awful person." Reba's dimpled smile disappeared. "It wasn't until he grabbed my cell phone . . . that's when I knew something was terribly wrong. I never even imagined he was looking for you, wanted to kill you."

Marla empathized with the visible shiver of revulsion shuddering across Reba's shoulders. "I'm just grateful the police showed up at Ed's place when they did," she confessed.

"That should teach you gals a lesson," was Naomi's unsympathetic

148

admonition. "Beware of good looking strangers. By the way," she focused her attention on Marla. "Speaking of strangers, what about that sea captain, the one who was supposedly dead, what's his name?'

"Mallory," Marla savored the name upon her lips. "Jacob Mallory."

"Oh, yes, Captain Mallory. What happened with him? Was he involved at all in that crab poaching? Like, wasn't it his boat being used?"

"Yes, but Jacob was entirely exonerated by Victor's confession," Marla explained, welcoming the opportunity to speak openly of the man whose memory she'd carried with her from the Cape, a man who seemed to have taken permanent residence in her thoughts, both waking and sleeping. "Victor admitted to using the Sea Nymph without Jacob's knowledge, then hoped to divert suspicion by destroying the boat along with its captain. Once he was faced with the charges of attempted murder, he willingly supplied the names of his accomplices, totally clearing Jacob. Of course," she added. "I think my deposition may have helped in settling the case, too."

"You're lucky your deposition was enough. A trial could have been endless." Wineglass in hand, Naomi moved toward the kitchenette for a refill. "You might still be stuck in that little fishing village," she admonished over her shoulder.

"Yes, yes, I suppose." Marla agreed fingering the knotted fringe of the afghan draped across her lap. Looking up, she met Reba's sympathetic glance and felt her face flush with the knowledge her friend deciphered the wistful response.

"What will become of your captain, now?" Reba inquired softly. "With his boat gone, his cabin burned . . .?"

"Theirs is a very close community," Marla offered, attempting to infuse her voice with objectiveness of a disinterested observer. "They look after their own. I understand the villagers plan to help Jacob build a new cabin, though I'm not sure it will be up on the bluff." Marla hesitated realizing she was divulging more than casual interest and hoped her faux pas hadn't been noticed.

"Of course, not everybody in the village gets along," she rallied. "I understand it was a heated argument with a customer over the ingredients of the lobster chowder that prompted Ruthie to just up and walk out on her waitress job at Mo's".

"And his boat," Reba refused to be distracted. "How will your captain make a living now, with his boat gone?"

"I suspect he'll work off the other fishing boats until he can get another one of his own." Marla gathered a sip of courage from the pale amber liquid in her own glass. "The tenacity of those people is absolutely amazing."

Noami returned from the kitchen, her glass of Vouvrey refreshed. "Well, I'm certainly glad it's all over. I'm sorry now I insisted on going to the Cape. We should have gone to Spain, like you wanted, Marla. In fact," she condescended, "you can choose our next destination, no arguments, no questions." She lifted her glass in salute. "So, gals, here's to Marla and our next vacation, wherever she may take us."

Marla's mind replayed the image of a somber, dark–haired sea captain, hands jammed in his pockets; fisherman's cap pulled low over his eyes. Only this time, his eyes were warm with caring, a gentle smile playing at the corners of his mouth. Marla's heart fluttered at the memory of the soft invitation in his voice as he said his goodbye.

"I 'spose you'll be headin' back to Seattle, now."

She'd been surprised at the unexpected stab of panic at his words, the chilling tide of loneliness surging through her. The warmth of his hands, resting on her shoulders, seeped through the oversized shirt she'd commandeered as her own.

Jacob's hands moved up to cradle her face. "I'm thinkin', maybe there'll come a day you'll be wantin' to come back to the Cape." His voice, soft and husky, curled around her like warm gray smoke. "You're gonna find me right here, just waitin' for that day to happen."

In the next instant, she was in his arms, his lips pressing softly against hers.

Marla forced her attention back to where her two friends stood expectantly before her, wineglasses held high. Blinking back the tears stinging her eyelids, she forced a smile to her lips. Then, crossing her fingers on the hand she furtively slid beneath the protective shelter of the afghan, Marla raised her own glass, "Yes," she echoed softly, "here's to our next vacation . . . wherever it may take us."

THE END

Printed in the United States
by Baker & Taylor Publisher Services